The Judge's Chambers
AND OTHER STORIES

The Judge's Chambers
AND OTHER STORIES

Lowell B. Komie

ACADEMY

CHICAGO

In 1983, nine of the stories in this collection were published in a paperback edition entitled *The Judge's Chambers* by the American Bar Association, the only time in its history that the American Bar Association has published a collection of fiction.

All stories in this collection appeared in *Student Lawyer,* the magazine of the Law Student Division of the American Bar Association, with the exception of "The Butterfly," published in *Kansas Quarterly,* "Picasso Is Dead," published in *The Hyde Parker,* and "Mentoring," previously unpublished. "The Cornucopia of Julia K" has been reprinted in *Canadian Lawyer.*

Published in 1987 by
Academy Chicago Publishers
425 North Michigan Avenue
Chicago, Illinois 60611

Copyright © 1987 Lowell B. Komie

Printed and bound in the USA

No part of this book may be reproduced
in any form without the express
written permission of the publisher.

Library of Congress Cataloging-in-Publication Data

Komie, Lowell B.
    The judge's chambers.

    1. Lawyers—Fiction.   I. Title.
[PS3561.0454J8   1987]   813'.54   86-32271
ISBN 0-89733-248-2
ISBN 0-89733-247-4 (pbk.)

For our family

CONTENTS

I AM GREENWALD, MY FATHER'S SON

He had brought them back from the rental gallery of the Art Institute. The paintings hung on the wall facing his desk, and already he could feel the warmth from the colors, vivid reds and oranges and yellows, soft earth colors, abstract whorls that spun in sensuous patterns. He had grouped the paintings around an oval collage of Bets and the children.

He particularly liked one picture, a large watercolor and ink sketch of a group of angels carrying a shrouded figure of a woman. It was named *The Assumption of St. Catherine of Alexandria*. The angels were flat–faced Oriental princesses, almost Byzantine, and their robes were elegantly embroidered red silk, filigreed with half moons and asteroids. The figure of St. Catherine was also flat-faced, with high cheekbones, and black vacant pinpoints for eyes. She was enshrouded in gray muslin, and the supporting angels flew with her corpse and held her gently like litter bearers. Below the angels were the rooftops of ancient Alexandria, tiny houses, cubes of ivory done in bright sun colors of the ancient desert. When he looked from his desk across the room at the painting, he often imagined himself standing in the hills overlooking some exotic port city, looking down at the water and at the harbor. He knew though that he would never make it out of Chicago.

Carter Greenwald was a partner in the firm of Kelly Heifetz, Greenwald, Baugh & Vonier, a firm of eighty-seven lawyers with offices on the thirty-fifth, thirty-sixth, and half of the thirty-seventh floors of the old Chicago Midland Exchange Building. The firm was celebrating its centennial year and had been founded just after the Civil War by John Kroft and William Greenwald, Carter's great grandfather. Old William Greenwald had been succeeded by his only son, Peter S., Carter's grandfather, and then William Carter Greenwald II, Carter's father, who had died last year after fifty years of practice with the firm. Carter had been a partner for ten years and had moved from the trial department, to antitrust, to labor, and now probate. He was still a junior partner though, his share of the firm profits (%.75693) churned out by the computer biweekly in the form of a flat white envelope containing a check for $1,250. This was augmented by another flat white computer envelope placed on his desk by the office manager on Christmas Eve day of each year with an additional two to eight thousand dollar bonus voted by the firm's executive committee. It was enough to live well, and he maintained a home in Winnetka, an old, white clapboard house on a ravine lot with his wife Betsy, two children, three dogs, one beat-up Chevy wagon, a new, steel-gray Volvo wagon that he had bought partly financed, and a sleek, purple XKE Jaguar racing coupe he had quietly acquired with some of the cash from his father's estate.

It was obvious to his partners that Carter didn't have the drive of W.C. II, his father. He had the old man's dark, intense face though and the familiar tall, angular body. But Carter's father had been a competitor, a slashing, combative man who loved litigation and who could sense an opponent's weak spot and lead a trial group of juniors to victory. He was a true legal general, a man who could argue and win a complex antitrust case or a proxy fight. He had been a member of the boards of many of the city's largest corporations. Above all, he was a businessman, shrewd and talented in fee setting and the gathering and currying of clients. The old man had been hard and concise and profane; the son, although willingly joining the firm after Yale Law School, seemed destined to slip gradually down the same ladder that his father had climbed. The younger man didn't have the stomach for the combat of trial work. He liked the travel associated with labor law, but he soon grew tired of motels and planes and being away from his family. He wasn't good at negotiating contracts with tough union negotiators. He found antitrust boring except for research. He enjoyed preparing memorandums, working late in the library, his books piled high around him, a young secretary from the pool staying late. He thought that some of the briefs he had written in the appellate section of antitrust had been good. The firm had even bound some in Moroccan leather and had shelved them in the glass bookcases that were reserved for work the partners considered distinctive. Several times lately, when he'd been down late at the office and only the scrub women were with him in the library, Carter would open the glass case and remove the three slim volumes that bore his name inscribed in gold on the binding, "C.P. Greenwald." The language of the briefs, though, brought no real feeling of accomplishment. The subjects were esoteric, the words not concerned with life. They were the dead words of a technocrat.

Perhaps he should just leave. Go out West, a small town in Colorado or Wyoming, hang up his shingle, put his feet up on a desk and deal with people. Perhaps be an Indian law specialist, traveling to tribal courts, adjusting disputes, occasionally flying to Washington to argue before the Supreme Court.

Perhaps he should learn a craft. Like glass blowing. He had seen a young man once, in Door County, Wisconsin, a young bearded glass blower who had an open furnace in a barn on an abandoned farm. Carter and Bets and the children had watched an exhibition at night, the young man using his glass blower's tube like a wand in the moonlight, his shadow dancing in the glow of the kiln, his face alive and infused with the mystery and magic of his craft. The young man had touched something alive with his hands. It was the same feeling that Carter tried to find with his briefs, but the triumph had eluded him.

Now he was stuck in the probate section. He'd been there for the past three years. But at least here things were orderly, and Carter was good at drawing his wills and trusts. The language was precise, and he would draft and redraft his instruments until he was certain that he had honed them down to white bone, like finely rubbed scrimshaw. He was a good draftsman, but the firm had recently bought three automatic typing machines to reproduce standard estate instruments. If you needed a Marital A and B Trust, you could slip in a precoded card and the typewriters would whir out the trust, perfectly typed. The whole procedure took about ten minutes. Since the machines were purchased, Carter was hardly doing any drafting at all. He'd probably drafted only four wills in the last three months and had dragged those jobs out as long as he could with hours of unnecessary tax research. He still met with clients though, and now, with the machines emptying his life, he looked forward to the personal contact. He was particularly good with little old ladies and represented the firm at luncheons given by bank trust departments for wealthy widows who were clients of the firm. He was good at sitting at these luncheons in dark panelled rooms up in the bank towers. He knew what to say and when to be quiet. He did not have to be told that the old ladies were important to the firm. They controlled their husbands' estates. The banks received annual commissions as trustees and the firm annual fees as attorneys for the trustees. He was paid to be circumspect, and he kept his mouth shut as he sat at the tables with the silver candelabras in the luncheon rooms. He would nod and sip his consommé and only occasionally accept one of the after luncheon cigars, cautious not to blow smoke and offend the widows. He saved the cigars for his office and the long afternoons facing him.

Lately, in the afternoons, with his office door closed, Carter had begun to compile a list. It was his list of what he thought was going wrong at the office, and tangentially, going wrong with his life. One of the children had brought home a purple grease-point pen from school, and Carter snitched the pen and brought it down on the train to his office and began the list, writing on a yellow legal pad in vivid purple ink.

This afternoon, Carter had returned from another luncheon at one of the bank trust departments and had quietly closed his office door and hung up his jacket. He removed an old telescope from the wall cabinet above his desk and trained the scope on the lake's harbor until he caught a freighter with rust on its sides, a tricolor flying at its stern, and two men in berets and heavy quilted jackets standing at the rail, smoking in the gray December afternoon. He tried to focus on their faces, but he couldn't catch them. The freighter was moving slowly along the breakwaters, and he followed it until it was lost behind the window frame. Then he shut the scope and pulled the curtains. He lit the cigar he had saved from the luncheon and sat back in his desk chair, his feet on the desk. After a moment, he looked up at the painting of St. Catherine, hoping the mosaic of the housetops would soon unscramble into his familiar dream. St. Catherine's eyes were slanted even though shut in death. The eyes had a particular cant, a familiar configuration. And so did the angels' faces, the faces done in the same deep rose color of the intricate robes. There was no expression in the faces though, not even the slightest trace of life in the faces.

Carter lifted his phone. "No calls, please," he said gruffly to the operator. The dream wouldn't come, so he began to look over his list. He began to read, his horn-rimmed half-glasses down on his nose.

Office and Other Problems C.P.G., was the title. Then he had drawn a thin purple line through that and had written, A Memorandum to All Partners—Matters of Concern in Firm Administration C.P.G., and again a line through that, changed to, Memorandum to All Partners re: Problems of Firm Administration C.P.G., and then finally another deletion and a change simply to, Office Memorandum C.P.G.

OFFICE MEMORANDUM C.P.G.

To All Partners:

For some time I have been troubled by certain matters in the routine of the firm and have not spoken out. I have concluded to remain silent no longer. There are many items of daily annoyance that I think could be (must be) eliminated or changed. I have drafted this memorandum for the purpose of calling your attention to those things that I find particularly distressing. I would like to discuss them further at a meeting of the Managing Committee that I propose be held within one week. The items are as follows:

Bells—The matter of the constant sounding of bell chimes when a lawyer cannot be reached on his office phone. I feel like Pavlov's dog being called to the phone. My particular signal is dong, dong, ding (pause two seconds) dong. I have no particular bitch with the alliteration. But I do feel like we're all trapped in a large department store. This constant chiming.

Brown Bagging in Offices—I notice that many of the older associates are now bringing lunch to the office. They eat with their office doors open in full view of clients and partners who pass along the corridors.

The odor of fruit and sandwiches can be detected outside their rooms. This simian practice should be immediately discontinued.

Time Sheets—Each day the assistant office manager places a "Daily Time Sheet" at my desk. I'm expected to fill it out and turn it in the following morning before I receive a fresh sheet. I dislike having to enter every phone call I make, i.e., "Call to Smith 1/4, Call to Jones 1/4." Can each phone call possibly take a quarter of an hour? Perhaps a fairer method of billing a client would be to have a glass full of sand at the lawyer's desk and as a call is made the sand glass could be tilted to flow down into a special receptacle. At the end of each day the total volume of sand could be picked up by the assistant office manager who would then carefully weigh it. I also am beginning to develop less tolerance for the cross hatches and grids on the time sheets that divide each day into hours and fractions of hours. The lines remind me of fourth grade mimeos brought home by my children. Calendars of school events drawn with a shaky stylus.

Floorboards—The floorboards in the corridors squeak. New carpet padding should be purchased. There is also an awful creaking on the interior stairways and the stairway carpeting is worn in several places. Certainly the bottom step leading to the library floor looks as pitted as the surface of Mars.

Rolling Pennies on Library Bookshelves—I'm sure our library is one of the most extensive private collections in the city. Often when I go down there (on the threadbare stairway carpet) the librarian and his assistant are rolling pennies along the vinyl tops of the bookcases. Admittedly, the librarian and his assistant are young law students and part-time employees, but they should be advised that their games are out of order. They should be made to sit at their desks. Also, they neglect to wear their gray dust jackets. They should be required to wear these jackets.

Computers and Auto-Types—The computer is surely a monster. All the lights blinking and ratchets and spools whirring. *Destroy* it. *Destroy* it before it destroys me. At least hang some rattan matchstick shades over the glass partitions surrounding the computer room. This monster (aided by the Executive Committee no doubt) has computed my partnership percentage at .75693. My God, by whose autocratic fiat am I, Carter Greenwald, human being, to be forever .75693? For God's sake move me up to 1.00000 percent and be done with it. At least then I won't have to invade my patrimony if Bets and I want to fly out to Aspen. And the auto-types . . . they're doing me out of a job. Smash them with a sledge. What do they know about the Rule Against Perpetuities? I can extemporize, the machines can't. I've read Moynihan's hornbook. Could an auto-type write this memorandum? You are turning us all into dying technocrats, dry little old men, servile and dyspeptic.

Firm Letterhead—The paper is too thin and has too parchmenty a feel. The watermark is too prominent and is visible in weak light. It's like the crested paper of a deluxe French hotel. I don't like the battery of names on our stationery and the arrangement of partners not by alphabet but by prominence within the firm. I am forty-second in the pecking order. Why? Why should Carter Greenwald be a thin engraved smudge of ink in a roster? I am alive and I have needs and my family has needs. We have human concerns. The lines of partners' names look like a mass obituary.

And the names of deceased partners on the right side trail down the edge of the paper like the footprints of little black mice. It's as if a pack of mice had scampered over our stationery, their tiny feet inked and leaving impressions everywhere. Why not just print the name of the firm across the top. "Kelly, Heifetz, Green-wald, Baugh & Vonier." Neatly engraved. No partners' names, no associates, no deceased partners, no one "Of Counsel," no Washington or Los Angeles Office. Just the firm name, address, and telephone number.

Office Softball Team—Gentlemen should not play softball. We are gentlemen. Our profession is a learned profession. Why softball? Who ordered the shirts with "KHGB&V" in a scroll across the front? I can't stand seeing the young jocks from the trial department with their gloves and bats on soft June afternoons.

CCH Reports—Who's filling the binders? The last Report Letters are often four to six weeks old. These services cost us thousands, tens of thousands. They must be kept up. Who's in charge of keeping up? (Another reason for lighting a fire under the librarians.) There's a high pile of CCH envelopes rising unopened on their desks. Open up the the goddamned envelopes, librarians! Stop rolling pennies!! The decimal nota-tions on the CCH reports remind me of my partnership percentage. Decimals, decimals, despair, despair.

Magazines and Periodicals—It's the routing and initialing. The defiling of perfectly good glossy covers of these publications with the insane scrawl of partners' initials. Why should I get my *Taxes* magazine with sets of initials on the right edge? TT, FDJ, KPT, to which I am required to add CPG and then pass the periodical on to JKM? Why the routing? And why the initialing? Don't you trust me to read? I read. And while we're on magazines, who chooses them for the reception room table? *Fortune, U.S. News and World Report, Nation's Business, The Economist, Dow Jones Magazine . . .* why not the *New Republic* or something racy like

Penthouse, something compact like that new little *Penthouse Forum* with the satyrs on the cover?

Switchboard Operators—As I pass the switchboard room all I hear is the rising murmur . . . "Kelly, Heifetz, Kelly, Heifetz." It's like a litany, some ancient liturgical chant, this answering of the phone with the greeting "Kelly, Heifetz, Kelly, Heifetz." At least have the operators say "Good Morning," or "Good Morning, Kelly, Heifetz." This constant "Kelly, Heifetz" chant, it's almost mesmerizing , to me at least, as I pass the operators, their pallid faces with black cups on their ears, cups blotting out life sounds, brown wisps of hair gone to gray under the steel bands of head sets, lips pursed and whispering "Kelly, Heifetz . . . " Why not "Hare Krishna, Hare Krishna"? Dress them in saffron robes. Better yet, why not "Kelly, Heifetz and *Greenwald*"? I am Greenwald. My father's son.

Pro Bono Work—In the past few years by vote of the Executive Committee, four Associates and two Partners have been assigned to Pro Bono work. Can't we construct a private entrance for our Pro Bono clients? How do I explain the presence of people in working clothes to my suburban widows dressed in black silk suits from Saks? Also, our Pro Bono lawyers are badly in need of haircuts.

Christmas Gifts—I find the giving of Christmas gifts of liquor to court clerks and clerical employees in the County and Federal buildings rather suggestive, if not a form of bribery. The cache of brightly wrapped packages of bottles in the storeroom appearing two weeks before Christmas, while attractive and festive, hardly seems in keeping with our role as seekers of justice, keepers of the law. There's a certain transference in political gift giving. The donor ultimately winds up smitten with the disease of the donee, a laying on of hands, a transmutation.

Charitable Donations—I am embarrassed on July evenings when I study my concert program by candle-light in the grass at Ravinia and I see the name of our firm listed as a donor. Oh, I know that all the major firms are listed, our competitors, but they, at least, are in the thousand dollar category and we're five hundred dollar donors. There I am, seated at a table on the lawn with our friends, dining elegantly with silver service, our faces aglow in the candle shadowing. I await the opening notes of the concert and tremble that our penury will be unmasked. Either up the donation to a thousand or get out of the book. Either support art or abandon it. Don't denigrate it.

Personal Notes.

T.S.S.—Don't search for me on the commuter train. I don't enjoy your company. You advise on crosswords. I know the Italian word for work is "opera." Your breath is bad. I can't abide a discussion of collaps-ible corporations when all I want to do is look out the window at vague shapes. Your preciseness has become intolerable. Why do you wear an Astrakhan in spring? Wholly to be a fool?

O.N.D—We say good night to each other, you say "take care." Can't you simply say, "good night"? "Take care" of whom, what? "Take care" of you? You seem to be doing a good job of that. "Take care" of myself? Isn't that implied by my very being, my *esse,* so to speak? Are you suggesting I require a Conservator? Will you act without fee? You who were once Order of the Coif, in-sisting on chutney for the Christmas party?

W.E.B.—You have a silver tea service on a rolling cart in the anteroom of your office. Your secretary serves coffee to clients and uses tongs with the cubes. A replica of your law school seal is framed in purple satin over the tea set, "Sanctus Ivo, Patronus Advocatorum— Bon Droit Et Raison." You pretentious bastard—with your Gucci loafers and tassels. I've seen you dictating to a hand set on your way to the office from Union Station. Someday that oppressed woman who tongs your cubes will drive a letter opener between your shoulder blades.

H.J.L.—Good and worthy man. Why a buzzer on your wristwatch? Time passes soon enough.

A.K.N.—Trial lawyer of note. Your depositions are as tedious and arcane as *The Canterbury Tales.* Must you wear cleats on your heels? All the juniors in your trial section are now wearing heels with cleats. Your team. All glen plaids from Brooks and scissored haircuts. "Sanctus Ivo, Patronus Advocatorum." Old black men limp into your offices to shine your shoes. You flip them quarters.

Greenwald stopped reading and took the purple grease pen and added the initials C.P.G. to his personal notes. What should he say about Carter P. Greenwald? C.P. Greenwald? He put the pen down and picked up a dart and looped it at a cork bull's-eye target that hung in a corner of the office. The dart landed with a thwack sound and quivered and fell to the floor. He closed his eyes and tried to remember himself as a law student. The class picture, he stands at the end of the first row, 1954, in the courtyard of Yale Law School, his Harris tweed jacket unbuttoned, trousers just a touch short, not breaking on his shoe tops but nevertheless knife-creased

khakis. Where had he gone wrong? He should never
have returned to Chicago. He could have stayed in New
Haven, or perhaps gone out West to try jury cases. In
twenty years he had never tried a jury case. He'd
become a businessman, not a lawyer. A corporate hand-
maiden. Assuaging old ladies for commissions. He could
have been a defender of the poor. Had a storefront office. The word L A W Y E R in block letters on the window. Late in the afternoon the shadows of L A W Y E R
would reflect back through the glass and bend along his
desk or across his face as he advised some working man,
using his Spanish 31, "Hola, amigo, yo soy abo-
gado. . . . " A B O G A D O . In Tucson. In a storefront
near the university. "C. Greenwald, A B O G A D O",
the letters bending in soft shadow over his desk. He had
never faced a man accused of crime. Talked to a man
behind bars. Argued for a man's liberty. Yo Soy
A B O G A D O . Sanctus Ivo. He could have at least
tried being a Federal Defender. One of his classmates
had offered him an appointment, but the Executive
Committe had prohibited it in 1970; they didn't want
partners doing Pro Bono.

He got up from the desk and pulled open the curtains again. The gray winter mist was floating up to him
now, shrouding the city as the figure of St. Catherine
was shrouded in the painting. He tugged the window
wide open and looked down. The left side of his head
seemed to be filled with the same grayness, the fog of
the city winter reaching into him, seeping, as if the gray
shroud of St. Catherine were folding over him. He
stared at the painting. Those vacant pin points of eyes.
The Byzantine faces. Red-faced angels in their elegant
robes. The rooftops of Alexandria, ivory cubes and

triangles. He reached for another of his darts and dropped it through the open window down to the empty courtyard thirty-five floors below. It disappeared, whirling into the murk.

The litter of angels with the slanted faces waited. Arrayed in their red robes. The covey of angels called to him in the soft call of angels, whispering " . . . Sanctus Ivo . . . Sanctus Ivo." He could place one foot on the sill and then another and sit down and slowly lower himself out, and then roll into the outstretched arms of the angels. It would be easy. It would be comforting.

He sat down on the sill with his back to the window and held another dart to his heart. He could see himself in his first year contracts class. The highly varnished student's desk. The arched gables of the lecture hall. The dry, professorial tones of the lecturer, the finger hovering on the seating chart. "Ah . . . Ah . . . Mr. Greenwald . . . where do you find the mutuality of obligation in this situation . . . Ah, Ah . . . Mr. Greenwald, is the consideration flowing to the offeree actual or illusory in the case at hand?" He held the dart and flicked its feathered fins with the nail of his right index finger. "Sophistry," he should have answered. "Mr. Greenwald, are you being facetious?" A tittering in the classroom. "Teach us to be lawyers, sir. I have come here to become a lawyer. How do I become a lawyer?"

He looked up at his framed oval collage of photographs of Bets and the children and then slowly he lowered himself down from the window sill and closed the window and pulled the curtains. He went over to his desk, sat down, and turned on his dictaphone. The red nodule glowed "on," he stared at it, it seemed to recess deep into his brain, like a ruby on a genie's turban, only

burning into him and glowing into his head, filling him
with its redness as it burrowed into him. His hand
reached for his memorandum. He wanted to begin dictating into the machine. He knew he couldn't write the
section about C.P.G. He tried to speak. The words
wouldn't come. His tongue was being cleaved by the red
nodule, a glowing diamond drill, cleaving his tongue
and paralyzing his speech. He put the papers down and
reached for the purple grease pen. Mute, his tongue not
working, slowly, laboriously he printed the letters on his
forehead. He wrote L A W Y E R . Then he began to cry.

THE INTERVIEW

She was tired of the interviews. She already had had twenty at law school and two flybacks, and so far no one had made her a summer job offer. Tonight, on her second flyback, she'd taken a bus from Washington National to Baltimore and checked into the hotel at 10:30 with her interview at Reavis & Ferris set for 11 a.m. So what could she do tonight? She had $20, her return ticket to Madison, and a VISA card with $285 charged on a $300 credit limit. She could go downstairs and sit in the bar.

She laughed at the face she saw in the mirror. Why not? Susan, you don't have to be that self-punishing, why not just go down and sit in the bar and have a drink? If a man approaches you, you can either tell him that you're a therapist or a nun, certainly not a second year law student. She touched her lashes with mascara and rubbed in a shade of lavender eye shadow. Someone had once told her that she had seeds of sunlight in her eyes. Who had said that? Was it Paul? No, Paul never said anything about her eyes. No one had ever told her that, she just dreamed that someone had told her that. She squinted her eyes and rubbed in the lavender shadow. She liked setting herself up this way. All right, if not a nun tonight, at least Anna Karenina.

She decided to have a drink at a table in the dining

room. The room was old and classic, waiters in formal dress, starched white tablecloths, sparkling glassware, and crystal chandeliers. She ordered a glass of white wine and looked around. She'd phoned her roommate before she left the room, and Tracy told her there'd been a call from Bartholomew & Gross in Indianapolis. That could mean she'd finally had an offer. She sipped the wine. Would Anna Karenina accept a summer job in Indianapolis? Of course she would.

A man was staring at her, a man with a beard, sitting alone. She glanced at him for a moment. He was nice-looking. She'd been thinking about Tax this morning. Why did Professor Marcus always wear the same pair of thick-soled shoes? They looked like orthopedic shoes. Marcus had eyes like a jellyfish, bulging and filled with sadness. She'd been called on and she hadn't been prepared. "Miss Eliofson?" "Pass." she'd said. "Mr. Brownstein?" "Pass." "Miss Allen?" "Pass." "Miss Oberweis?" "Pass." "All right," Marcus had said, "four passes. It doesn't seem that there's a high level of preparation. Who has the case?" Someone's hand shot up. How could she be prepared if she was always running off to the interview room? She had tried to brief a few cases last night in the library, but there were so many undergraduates talking and laughing that she'd left and gone over to Paul's, but she couldn't find him. Why hadn't he waited for her? It seemed that he was never there anymore for her when she needed him. She wanted to be with him last night, and he hadn't even left a message for her, just his scabrous cat staring at her with its flat amber eyes.

The man was looking over at her again and now he was standing.

Who was Anna Karenina's lover? Count Vronsky? Did Count Vronsky have a brown beard?

Suddenly the man walked to her table.

She didn't say anything and instead nodded her head.

"What does that mean," he asked, "yes or no?"

"Yes, sit down. I'm not waiting for anyone."

"My name is Steven Wainwright."

"My name is Anna."

"May I ask your last name?"

"Yes. Karen."

"Would you like some champagne, Anna Karen?"

An hour later they were both very drunk on champagne, and were standing in the Baltimore Aquarium staring at a fish. Steven was an SEC lawyer from New Orleans and he insisted on showing her the lawyer fish at the Baltimore Aquarium.

"Is that really a lawyer fish?" she said, watching the huge black fish with the bulging eyes in the glass case. It looked like Professor Marcus. "Where's his briefcase?"

"How can you be certain it's a he?"

"Okay, where's *her* briefcase?" She puffed out her cheeks and imitated the fish.

The lawyer fish was huge. It looked prehistoric with a black body and fat gray mottled underbelly. It blinked at Susan and languidly moved one huge fin.

"Why do they call it the lawyer fish?" She looked at him.

"Because it looks like a lawyer. Can't you see it's wearing glasses and has a vest with a key chain?"

She pointed to the plaque, "Lawyer Americanus," and burped. She was very giddy and dizzy from the champagne. "What will you give me if I dive into its tank?"

"A hundred dollars."

"All right, let's see it."

Steven took out his wallet and removed a crinkled $100 bill. "I always save this for a contingency."

She took off her jacket and handed it to him, and climbed up the ladder at the side of the tank. "How do I know he won't bite me?" she called down to Steven, looking over the rim at the fish. "It's full of slime! I can't do it! Do you think it eats people?"

"No, it's perfectly harmless. Why don't you give him the hundred-dollar bill and see if he eats it?"

She looked down again at the lawyer fish. She *could* do it. She could just step out of her skirt and blouse and slowly lower herself down into the tank. How would she get out, though? She saw a ledge of stairs leading into the tank which must be used for feeding. Was she drunk enough to do this? She stepped out of her skirt and tossed it at Steven. She unbuttoned her blouse and fluttered it down to him, and suddenly she was in the water, lowering herself down into the tank. The water was almost tepid. She felt like she had fallen into consommé. Holding her nose, she fell to the bottom and stood searching for the lawyer fish. It was too murky and she couldn't see the fish. Then she saw the huge shadow in the corner of the tank. She stared at it. Should she touch it? She could always say she had touched a lawyer fish. It seemed to sense that she was in the tank, but it made no motion toward her. She reached out and touched its side. She was beginning to run out of breath. She watched the slowly undulating fin. The two hooded eyes peered at her. She had to have some air, so she kicked through the murky water over to the ladder and thrust herself up the slippery rungs and gasped for air.

"I should never have done that," she said, gasping to Steven. "I can't believe I really did that. Did I actually do that?"

Back at the hotel they had a drink at the bar before they said goodnight. She bought the drinks with Steven's $100 bill and except for her stringy wet hair, no one would have known she had been to the bottom of the tank to visit the lawyer fish.

They exchanged addresses and phone numbers on cocktail napkins and he led her into a side room near the elevator and kissed her goodnight. He had soft lips, and she liked kissing him, and when the elevator doors closed, he looked at her sadly because they knew they would never see each other again.

"What is the one thing in the world you want, Anna?" he had asked her.

"I want a dog. I want a dog to love me. Men are too deceitful. When I was in high school, I had a tiny dog named Jacques and I used to keep him in my desk drawer and do my homework over him."

The last thing he said to her was, "A woman who can go into the tank with the lawyer fish doesn't belong in the corporate army."

In the room she took a shower and washed the dirt off and shampooed her hair. She wrapped herself in the big white terrycloth robe the hotel provided and dumped all the plastic bottles of shampoo and body lotion in her purse; then she called Paul in Madison. No answer. Maybe he was with someone. No, he was probably out for a beer with his roommate. Steven's lips had been soft, and she liked his eyes. What did he mean by the corporate army? Why had she gone into the tank with that ugly fish? Would she dream of it? No, she wouldn't allow herself to dream about it.

In the morning she dressed in her gray suit, and after she put on her makeup and brushed her hair, she called her roommate. She wore a white silk blouse with a lace collar and a golden sun-god costume jewelry pin with tiny red jeweled eyes. She tried it first on her lapel and then at her throat. She pinned it at her throat.

It was 9 in Baltimore, too early to call the firm in Indianapolis. Her interview was at 11. She had breakfast in the coffee shop off the lobby, and then took a walk and looked at some of the shop windows. In the window reflection she looked like any other eastern yuppie with her lace collar and sun-god pin. She'd put last night and the gray fish out of her mind.

When she returned to the room she thought of calling Paul again. He could have tried to reach her last night and not have left a message. Before she called him she made sure by ringing the desk.

"What is your room number?"

"623."

"You are Susan Eliofson?"

"Yes."

"I'm sorry, no messages."

She hesitated for a moment and dialed Paul's number in Madison.

"Hello?" he answered in a sleepy voice.

"It's me."

"How's it going?"

"Okay. I tried to call you last night."

"I stayed late at the library and went out with some friends for a beer."

She attempted to sound casual. "Who were you with?"

"Oh, Michael and some of his weird friends. What did you do?"

"I just ate dinner and went to bed. I was really tired." She was quiet for a moment.

"Susan, are you still there?"

"Yes, I'm sorry."

"What time will you be back? I could meet you at the airport and drive you."

"I thought your car was broken."

"It was, but I fixed it last night."

"No, don't pick me up. I'll just take the bus."

"Okay, I'll see you tomorrow in class."

"You really sound weird, Paul."

"I'm just tired, Susan. I'm going back to bed. I'll miss Tax, but I don't care. See you."

She put the receiver down and went into the bathroom and looked at herself in the mirror. Susan, you're not freaked out, she said, touching her eyes on the mirror. Don't let him upset you. She unwrapped the plastic cover from the glass and sipped some cold water. She put on lip gloss and went back to the bed, sat down and called Bartholomew & Gross in Indianapolis.

"Mr. Krakauer, please."

"May I say who's calling?"

"Yes, Susan Eliofson from Madison." There was a pause and she looked at her watch. She still had almost an hour before the Baltimore interview.

"Krakauer."

"Hello, Mr. Krakauer. This is Susan Eliofson from the University of Wisconsin Law School returning your call."

"Oh yes, Susan. I guess I got your roommate. Susan, I'm sorry to bring you bad news. We're not going to make an offer."

"Oh."

"I'm awfully sorry. You really had good interviews with several of the partners, but we're cutting back on our hiring for the summer."

"I understand."

"I think you'll find that situation all over. I know several of the firms in Indianapolis are cutting back."

"Thank you, anyway."

"Again, I'm sorry. It was nice meeting you. I wish you luck. We've mailed a check for your expenses to you in Madison."

"Okay. Thanks a lot."

"Goodbye, Susan."

She took a cab to Reavis & Ferris and arrived 20 minutes early. The reception room was large and furnished in blond paneling with oil paintings of several men that she presumed were partners of the firm. There were two receptionists with practiced smiles and wearing silk blouses almost similar to hers. They offered her coffee or tea. They also gave her a notebook with a roster and photographs of all the partners and associates of Reavis & Ferris.

She began to leaf through the notebook. There were 125 lawyers, and only four women lawyers. No blacks, no Asians, no Latin names. Only one woman had made partner. She looked at her face. Elizabeth Moncrief. She was attractive. Gray-haired. Hobbies: "Traveling."

Education: "University of South Carolina, B.A., Columbia, LL.D." Marital status: "Single." She flipped the pages to another woman. Patti Monahan. Johns Hopkins, B.A., University of Virginia, LL.D. She looked about 24. Hobbies: "Bartending; ski bumming."

A young woman with hair frizzed in a wild perm came into the reception room and greeted her with a big smile and handshake. "Hi, I'm Missy Crandall. I work with John Raymond. I'm a legal assistant."

Susan stood, holding the firm roster.

"John asked that you come back to his office. I'll take you there. How do you like our yearbook?"

"It's very nice."

"It's just awful. One of the partners saw this in New York and came back and insisted we all pose, so we spent two months posing in shifts and writing our bios." She took the book from Susan and opened it to her photograph. "That's me, Missy Crandall—paralegal—real estate. Hobbies: men, and group therapy. Isn't that terrific? It's a good way to meet people as neurotic as yourself."

Susan smiled. They walked by several offices and each time the lawyer looked up at them without expression.

Missy opened the door to John Raymond's office and told Susan to sit down, he'd be with her in a moment. "Would you like another cup of tea?"

"No, thank you."

"Well, maybe a soft drink? John's a Pepsi freak."

"No, nothing, thank you."

"I'll meet you in the reception area."

"Do you like it here, Missy?"

"Oh, it's okay. I'm getting married, and we're moving to California, so I don't really think about the office. The money's good, and there are some nice people. We're always under tons of pressure, though."

John Raymond came into the office. He was a dark, sharp-faced, small man, about 35, in short sleeves and red suspenders. "Hi, you're Susan?"

"Yes."

"Okay. I'm sorry to have kept you waiting." The phone rang. "Excuse me," he said.

Susan felt something on her neck. She put her hand under her hair and she could feel something crawling along her neck, something slimy. She pulled it away from her neck and looked at it. It looked like a black beetle, then she recognized what it was. It was a leech, and two droplets of her blood were clinging to it. My God! She had showered and shampooed and she was covered with leeches! She quickly thrust her hand back around her neck and through her hair, but she didn't find another one. She took a piece of Kleenex, put the leech into it, and shoved it into her coat pocket.

"You'll crater that deal," Raymond was saying into the phone. He tapped on the mouthpiece with his pencil. "If you do that, Mitch, you'll crater the deal." He lit a cigarette. "I'll soldier for you, but I won't be a litter-bearer."

He looked at Susan, and she could feel her hand trembling. Suddenly he offered her a cigarette. She refused it.

"Yeah," he said. "I'm tracking you, Mitch. I said I'm tracking you. Okay, call me back with the numbers." He hung up. "So," he said to her without looking at her. He held his pencil over her resumé. "Why do you want to become a lawyer?"

They all ask that question first. She thought about the leech in the piece of Kleenex. She could hand it to him and leave. "I want to be a lawyer because I think it will be interesting and challenging."

"What will be interesting and challenging?" He was watching her hand.

"Being a lawyer."

"How do you know?"

"I'm presuming."

"Do you find law school interesting and challenging?"

"Not particularly. Occasionally I do."

"What courses are you interested in?"

"I like Corporations, I enjoy Contracts. Civil Procedure, I like Antitrust." She was giving him the answers she knew she should give, and now she was sitting on her right hand. She had the sensation that the leech had gotten out of the piece of Kleenex and was crawling up out of her pocket. She looked down at her pocket.

The phone rang again, and she saw a tremor on the left side of his face.

"Susan, I think that's enough. It's really a bad time for me. I'm trying to do a deal and be in Washington by 1:30. So why don't you go back out to reception and see Missy? She'll take you down the line." He stuck his hand out.

"Okay," he said into the phone, "Okay, Mitch, I'm still tracking you." He lit another cigarette and blew some smoke toward the ceiling, swiveling in his chair so his back was to Susan. "Bottom line, net net. You call out the numbers."

She went back to the reception room where Missy was waiting for her. "Well, how did it go?"

"I don't know. Is there a washroom here?"

"Sure, I'll get the key for you."

In the washroom she brushed her hair furiously. She checked her collar and pulled her blouse open and then sprayed her neck with cologne. She did her lips again, but her mouth seemed to leer at her in the mirror, red like the droplets of blood on the leech. She rubbed all her lipstick off and washed her face so she had no makeup at all. She did look like a young nun.

She thought of flushing the leech down the toilet, but instead she carefully uncoiled the Kleenex. The leech was dormant, like a slug clinging to the underside of a lily pad. She prodded it once with her finger and it moved. She rinsed the Kleenex with water and closed it around the leech and carefully put it back into her pocket. For some reason she wanted to keep it alive.

Peter Lindauer was immaculately dressed in a gray flannel pinstripe suit. His shoes were perfectly shined, and his hair was scissored in neatly cut layers. He picked up her resumé and blew on his glasses. She looked at his degree on the wall. He was a graduate of Harvard Law. Cambridgiensis. Cambridgiensis was a gerund. She wondered if Lindauer knew it was a gerund.

"What is your GPA now, Susan?"

"I think it's 2.5 or maybe 2.6."

He blew on his glasses again and held them up. "I didn't know we were flying back 2.5s. We never used to fly back under 3.0."

"I guess I just hit it off with your interviewer."

"I really didn't know we were interviewing under 3.0."

She was thinking of the white light in the waiting room at school. How many times had she sat in the room in Madison waiting for the light to signal that the previous student was through? Twenty times? Twenty-five times staring at the light? Then impatiently, almost always, a male voice. "Susan—Miss Eliofson—ah, yes, Susan. Please come in and sit down." As soon as she sat, the second or third question. "What's your GPA, Susan?" There was a tree that she would watch out the window when they asked the question, a small bare-branched tree. Still, she had two flybacks, even with her 2.5. One of the women with a 3.5 had twenty flybacks. She was the Queen of the Flybacks, and Susan wasn't even a princess.

Lindauer clicked his silver ballpoint pen. "What was your LSAT?"

"Twenty-five."

"About mid-level."

"Yes, mid-level."

"Well," he said, "I see you like underwater photography. Scuba diving."

"Yes. I'm interested in diving."

"Where have you been diving?"

"Oh, the Caribbean, the Florida Keys. Last night I visited the Baltimore Aquarium."

"You've seen our aquarium?"

"Yes. Do you know they have a lawyer fish there?"

"No, I didn't know."

"They do." She wondered if he would ask her what the lawyer fish's GPA was, but he didn't.

"Why do you want to be a lawyer, Susan?"

"I guess I want to feel like I'm participating in the system. I can probably do some good. Also, I'd like to make some money." She crossed her legs.

"If you could buy any kind of a car, Susan, what

kind of car would you buy?" He stared at her, expressionless.

"Probably a Porsche. A black Porsche."

"Do you know what your SAT score was?"

"My SAT? That must have been five years ago."

"Don't you remember?"

"No, I really don't remember."

The phone rang. He turned away from her. "Yes? Oh, hello, Richard. No, I've been trying to confirm our luncheon. Yes. Yes, at the dining room in the Belvedere. No, I can talk. I've just got someone here applying for a job. We're really through." He turned and his glasses flashed at her. "Susan, I'm sure we'll be in touch. Missy will be waiting for you in the reception room." He turned away from her. "Richard, I also want to talk to you about those hearings on the twenty-fifth. I think our approach is a little foolish. . . . "

She stood up. The sun was coming through the window in a circle of white light, like the light in Madison in the interview waiting room. She would never be the Queen of the Flybacks. Cambridgiensis. Our paternal school. Of course it was a gerund. What difference did it all make. She was so tired of the system. She just wanted to scream at him.

She reached into her pocket. His back was still turned. She unfolded the Kleenex and reached out to him and gently put the leech on the collar of his immaculate gray pinstripe suit. The leech immediately began to undulate toward his neck, crawling toward the golden hairs at the back of his neck. The golden pollen. The white lily.

"Excuse me," she said, "Peter."

He turned back toward her impatiently.

"Thank you," she said.

THE LOVES OF DAVID FREUND

When David Freund began at the firm of Gottfried, Oberleitter, Mandel, and Johnstone in the winter of 1953, it was as an assistant librarian after his morning classes at the University of Chicago Law School. He used to ride the Hyde Park Express three days a week to the edge of the Loop and then walk to work down Jackson Boulevard with his brown lunch bag. He particularly liked Gottfried, Oberleitter because of certain of its cachets: *The Australian Reports,* fully bound in blue leather and shimmering in the reception room; the blond receptionist, a divorceé of perhaps thirty-two, who wore angora sweaters and, when she swished through the swinging leather doors, left little wisps of angora floating in the dank corridors.

But the corridors of Freund's mind were even danker than the corridors of Gottfried, Oberleitter, and, at twenty-three, at long last the mystery of law school was beginning to unravel for him. In fact, now in his second year, he had acquired a patina of lethargy, bemusement, and scorn. He attended on other places and in other rooms. Women haunted him. Not really women, girls haunted him. And he had three.

One, a nurse at Billings Hospital near the university , was tall and pale-faced, morose and autocratic. She'd been manipulating Freund like a zany marionette. One night anger, the next night silence, the next night passion. Then she'd disappear for a week. Freund was convinced that she'd been carrying on a second love affair with a resident in surgery. In any event, Freund had no place to take her. Certainly not his room in the dormitory with two roommates. Freund slept in the lower of a double decker bunk. The upper occupant, Derick McMaster, seldom washed his clothes: they dangled from the upper bunk in a laundry bag that hung in Freund's face like a bulbous cloth pendulum. It would be extremely difficult to convince any of Freund's three loves to sneak into the dormitory up to his room, and, once there, it would be even more difficult to convince them to lie in Freund's lower bunk beneath McMaster's dangling scum bag. The odor would immediately dispel any notions of passion. So Freund had abandoned the idea as he had long ago abandoned his daily request to McMaster, "For Christ's sake, Derick, wash up."

David Freund's second woman was a teaching assistant at the University Lab School and a graduate student in English Lit. In her senior year, after a love affair with a Tibetan doctoral candidate who left her to assist in opening a lamasery in lower Manhattan, Freund met her. They made love only one time, and that was on the second night they dated and in the back seat of a stranger's car parked on Fifty-Fifth Street. Freund had been concerned that the owner might return at any minute and had hurried his lovemaking to such a crescendo that she denied for weeks that any physical contact between them had taken place. Moreover, two months after that night in the stranger's parked car, she denied that she'd even been there with Freund, though

he'd gently reminded her that they'd left a heart and initials traced in the vapor on the car window. Now, she
was barely speaking to him, and after ten more dates
had never again permitted him to do more than occasionally lie on top of her and feign the love act.
Freund, however, was still intent on seducing her.

Even though law school had taught Freund to be a
rationalist, he still had a predilection for girls in knee
socks and parked cars. He looked for cars parked deep in
the shadows of the private parking lots with electronic
gates. None of his girls had a place, they all lived in dor-
mitories or had roommates. His own dormitory room
was out of the question with McMaster and then, of
course, his other roommate, Marshall Bloomberg, of
Yonkers. Bloomberg had the disconcerting habit of
coming in drunk at midnight and then briefing his
morning cases naked at his desk while brewing exotic
teas on his hot plate. He would read his cases aloud, sip
his tea, moan, sweat, burp, curse, and belch. In short,
Marshall was a real pig. Even a hardened young woman, intent on defilement, would not yield to Freund in
that room with McMaster's scum bag and Bloomberg
looking on.

So Freund opted for the risks of a stranger's parked
car as opposed to McMaster and Bloomberg's turf. And,
on reflection, it was probably the more rational choice,
though any person in Hyde Park, even in the fifties,
upon opening his car door and finding strangers in the
back seat, might shoot first and then ask questions. But
Freund had never been caught and, therefore, had never
been shot.

The third woman in Freund's life, Alicia Montgomery-Stevens, was Freund's classmate and a law

review editor. Miss Montgomery-Stevens, though, re-
garded Freund with suspicion and, being the only woman in a class of thirty men, had developed a healthy
skepticism for any overtures of love or even friendship
proffered by her classmates. Montgomery-Stevens was
a loner. She was a lovely blonde, with green eyes, very
red lips, perfect skin, and large breasts. Also, she was
tall and rangy, and Freund, being short, dark, bearded,
and intense, was immediately attracted to the cool and
sophisticated Alicia. She wore corduroy skirts and
tweed jackets with hunting patches and cashmere tur-
tlenecks, and how he longed to slip his hand underneath
the cashmere. He sat in back of her in estate planning
and spent hours watching the configuration of the wings
of her backbones and the tracings of her slip straps.

Occasionally, when they'd both been studying late
at the library, he'd ask Alicia out for a beer and they'd
go to Jimmy's. They'd even met on a few Saturday
nights, and, last Saturday, he'd walked her home,
feverishly trying the doors of parked cars as they approached her dormitory.

"What are you doing, David?"

"Nothing."

"Why are you bumping up against the cars?"

"Am I? I'm sorry."

"Well, don't apologize to the cars."

"No, no. I'm apologizing to you."

"You must really be drunk."

"I'm not drunk, Alicia."

"Well, stop lurching up against the cars."

"Lurching? Am I lurching? I didn't think I was
lurching."

They stood for a moment in the winter moonlight

just before the entrance to her dormitory, and he took her into his arms and kissed her for the first time. She kissed him back and he buried his face in the fragrance of her hair, Miss Alicia Montgomery-Stevens, Articles Editor.

"Let's sneak up to your room, Lish."

"We can't."

"Why not?" He kissed her again and she was extremely passionate. "Why not?"

"Oh, David."

"Lish, we can. No one will see us."

"What about my roommate?"

"You have a roommate?"

"Of course I have a roommate." She pulled him to her again and this time she pushed herself up against him with all her strength and pressed her mouth on his lips. Her parents had given her a new fur coat for her birthday, and, while it made her look quite sophisticated, he felt like he was embracing a huge muskrat. The coat completely insulated her from any sense of Freund's intensity, and therefore it was an effective gift because it not only kept their daughter warm, but also chaste.

Freund's affair with Alicia, though, soon began to engage the curiosity of his classmates, particularly McMaster and Bloomberg. At lunch one afternoon, after hamburgers and coffee, Freund was trying to get them to resume their customary trivia game. They always started with what they called first-year trivia. It was a game designed to see how much they'd forgotten of their first-year courses.

McMaster sat there picking onions out of his teeth, Bloomberg was looking out the window for girls.

"Okay, Derick, what's the Doctrine of Worthier Title?" Freund asked, starting off the game.

"How you making out with Alicia?"was McMaster's reply.

"Alicia? What's the Doctrine of the Fertile Octogenarian?"

"Screw the Fertile Octogenarian. Tell us about Alicia."

"Yeah, tell about Alicia," Bloomberg said.

"Oh, come on, you guys. Forget Alicia."

"Does she like it?" Marshall Bloomberg asked Freund with a grin.

"I don't want to talk about her."

"You're just afraid we'll tell her and she'll cut you off," McMaster said.

"All right, Derick. The Rule in Shelley's Case. Give me the Rule in Shelley's Case."

"Shelley who?" Marshall Bloomberg grinned. "And does she have a roommate?"

Right then Freund knew he had to find a place. He had to consummate his love affair with Alicia before his roommates screwed it up. He knew that every relationship peaked and that he and Alicia were at the apogee. He was already on the downhill side with the nurse and the teaching assistant. Both of them were becoming increasingly more intricate and elusive. He knew by the way Alicia clung to him the last time they were together that now was the time to find a place.

So he began to look. At first he considered a motel. It was out of the question. He could never get Alicia to go to a motel. The parked car routine was too unreliable. There had to be a perfect admixture of her drunkenness, a decently warm evening, a car precisely placed with the doors left unlocked. It was a difficult and chancy mixture. It had worked once with the teacher, but Alicia was too smart and too tall and rangy for Freund to overcome either intellectually or physically. He couldn't see himself yanking Alicia into the back seat of an Oldsmobile, or even a Buick Roadmaster.

At this time in Freund's life, the senior partner of Gottfried, Oberleitter acquired a new couch. It was beige, a soft, nubby basket weave, with plump throw cushions. Freund noticed it immediately since he'd been summoned into Gottfried's office to dispose of the wrapping paper.

"New couch," Alfred Gottfried mumbled to the assistant librarian without looking up from the brief he was reading. He was a sharp-faced man in his mid-seventies with a thin toupee of brown hair and gold spectacles. "Mrs. Gottfried bought the damned thing. She wants me to take a nap after lunch."

"Yes, sir," Freund said.

"A ridiculous idea."

"I should think so," Freund said.

"What's that?" Gottfried snapped. He put his pencil down and looked up sharply at Freund. He reached for a small varnished wooden gavel that sat on a block on his desk and rapped it softly on his palm.

"The couch, sir. You said it was ridiculous."

"I said that?"

"I guess you didn't."

"Well, young man. Talk straight, think straight. Where do you go to law school?"

"The University of Chicago, sir."

"Certainly they teach you to think straight down there. Unless they've changed. I suppose eventually all those liberal notions bend your thinking." He paused, put the gavel down, picked up his pencil, and went back to work. Freund began to crinkle the packing paper. The couch was at the far end of Gottfried's cavernous office, up against a paneled wall, beneath the portrait of Gottfried's father, the dark-faced, heavy-browed founder of the firm. Freund carefully folded the paper and as he did so he tested the couch with his hand. It was very soft.

"Don't let them throw sand in your eyes, young man," Alfred Gottfried called from the other end of the office. It was his favorite expression. He always used it with a jury in his closing arguments.

"No, sir," Freund replied as he shut the heavy door. The door clicked shut.

"I won't," he said quietly.

At ten o'clock that Friday evening, Freund led Alicia into the dim corridor of Gottfried, Oberleitter, through the rear door on the thirty-fifth floor. They were both very drunk. They'd skipped dinner and had been drinking beer for three hours when Freund whispered to her that he had the key to the law firm.

They were giggling and bumping each other as they went down the hall leading to Gottfried's office. Alicia began doing a harem girl dance in the corridor lit by the blue night-light. She used her scarf as a veil and while Freund snapped his fingers, Miss Montgomery-Stevens did a bump and grind beneath the oil portrait of each deceased partner in the long paneled hallway. When they reached Alfred Gottfried's office, Alicia squealed when she saw the soft beige couch and Freund tackled her and they both fell rapturously into its cushions. Freund kicked his shoes off and then he took Alicia by the hand and walked her over to the windows behind Gottfried's huge desk. The tall buildings of Chicago's financial district were ablaze with light. For a moment, Freund and Alicia stood there, high above the lights of the city, and watched the traffic streaming. Then Freund began his own dance, shedding his clothes in the darkness. Alicia was still fully clothed. She stood beside him and unpinned her hair and then slowly took off her clothes and dropped them in a pile by the couch. They fell into the soft cushions, naked and laughing in each other's arms. Just then the desk lamp flicked on. Freund saw Alfred Gottfried at the far end of the room at his desk.

"Oh my God," Freund whispered to her.

"What, David?"

"Shhh!"

"David, what is it?"

"For God's sake, Alicia, it's the old man."

She sat up and stared.

There at the other end of the huge office was Alfred Gottfried seated at his desk in the dim light of the desk lamp.

"David."

"Just be quiet, Alicia. He doesn't see us."

Gottfried had come into the office through his private entrance door. They both watched the old man. Alicia slipped on her blouse and Freund wriggled into his trousers. They sat absolutely still on the couch under the founder's portrait.

Alfred Gottfried was looking through his desk for some airline tickets. He and his wife were flying to Caracas in the morning, and he'd left the damn tickets in his desk. So after a bon voyage dinner at his son's apartment, he had asked the chauffeur to stop off at the office. Now he'd found them and put the packet in his wallet. He leaned forward to turn off the desk lamp when he stopped and peered out into the room, his glasses flashing at them out of the circle of light. Gottfried suddenly walked around to the front of his desk. Alicia was shaking and Freund stroked her hair. Gottfried's shadow extended as he approached them. Suddenly he wheeled and turned and went into a closet at the other end of the room. He hadn't seen them.

When he emerged from the closet, he was dressed in a judge's gown and a white wig. He held the edges of the gown and pirouetted in front of his desk and sat down in his large leather chair. He reached for his gavel and rapped it on the wooden block. The hollow *thock* sound echoed in the cavernous room. He twirled in the desk chair and then stood before the windows overlooking the city. He looked like a mammoth bat with its wings spread. He lingered at the window for a few minutes, and then he disappeared back into the closet. When he came out he was dressed again in his waistcoat, overcoat, furled umbrella, and black homburg. He peered out once again into the room and then bent over the desk and pulled the chain of the desk lamp. He left through his private door.

David Freund padded up to the door, bare chested, dressed in his trousers, and listened to Gottfried's retreating footsteps as the old man went down the corridor.

"Oh, David!" she said from the couch.

"I know."

"I mean, can you believe that!"

"Just forget it," he whispered. "He won't be back. And I know he didn't see us."

David Freund returned to the couch and took Alicia in his arms. At last they were alone and Alicia pulled him to her and they made love hidden in the deep cushions of Gottfried's magnificent new couch. But they were subdued, awed somewhat by what they'd seen. After all, they had just made love in a judicial chamber, and as law students they had notions of decorum. On the way out, she didn't do her harem girl dance, and even though Freund was wearing the judge's wig, he'd return it before Gottfried came back from Caracas. He just wanted to show it to McMaster and Bloomberg.

THE CORNUCOPIA OF JULIA K.

It started in the elevator when the doors shut and she realized that she was standing there with her laundry and cleaning in her arms. She knew that she was in the elevator but she wondered why she was going up to her office carrying a box of laundry and a suit while all the men were pushing past her heading for court with their briefcases. She felt like she had fallen into some kind of time trough. Last week she'd been ten minutes late for everything. This week the trough had grown to twenty minutes, an irretrievable twenty minutes. The doors shut and Julia was alone. She hated cologne and tobacco odors first thing in the morning, and, as the elevator began to move, she already felt the pressure beginning to build behind her eyes.

The walk down the corridors of her law firm always reminded her of peering into the compartments of a doll's house, little people in the rooms, little stick furniture, people caught in frozen moments, blinking, looking up at her as she passed. There were nameplates beside each doorway. She had an immaculate nameplate, white enameled letters on a black plaque. Julia Latham Kiefer. Across from every office there was a stenographer's typing carrel formed by a curved, white plaster half-wall with hi-tech furniture and word-processing equipment. The occupant of the carrel was a woman, usually bent over a scanning screen. Julia had sent a memorandum to the office committee suggesting that the scanning screens emitted radiation and that the stenographers be issued radiation badges. She knew that the machines were cancerous, that the green glowing chains of perfectly formed calligraphy were as lethal as chains of carcinoma cells. It was all excess verbiage anyway, pages and pages of abstruse verbiage, and it was metastasizing and spilling out of the screens. Even the machines wouldn't store it anymore. It would eventually kill the women in the carrels. She thought about that this morning as she made the corridor walk.

When she entered her own office, she put the cleaning and laundry down and reached across and touched the asparagus fern on her bookcase. It was a very beautiful plant and she liked to touch its soft fronds as soon as she closed the door.

She'd told her psychiatrist about it.

"Every morning lately, before I do anything, I reach across to the plant and touch it."

"Maybe you're just acting something out, Julia."

"Acting out?"

"Well, psychodynamically. Like if I reach out and touch this leaf. What does it mean?" He touched the plant beside him.

"It means you're tired of listening to me, Norman."

"It could be something else."

"Such as."

"Such as I'm tired of being alone."

Julia touched her hair and slowly crossed her legs. She noticed that her hand was trembling as she reached for a cigarette.

"Do you think the plant will eventually abandon me, Norman?"

"I don't know, Julia. Do you water it enough?"

She'd laughed and laughed.

She remembered that conversation this morning. She also knew she was already fifteen minutes late for a conference of the plaintiff's committee on a securities case. Soon it would be twenty minutes.

There was a knock on the door. Her secretary, Claudia, slowly opened it and handed her a cup of black coffee. "Your mother is on the phone from Sarasota. She wants to know what flight."

"Don't tell her I'm here. Tell her I leave Chicago at 8:30. Look up the flight. The tickets are somewhere in this horrible pile. I'll call her from O'Hare before I leave."

She sipped the coffee and put it down and picked up her cologne atomizer and squirted it at the secretary. "Halston, Claudia," Julia said as she rushed by.

"Try a fragrance lift."

The cold air of LaSalle Street hit her face as she walked through traffic to the bank building across the street. She wore a long hooded raccoon coat with black cloth buttons edged with red glass jewels. In the Chicago gloom she looked like a wealthy young North Shore wife picking her way through the slush to meet her husband for a conference at the bank's trust department. Julia Kiefer at thirty-two was a litigator, a trial lawyer, and lead counsel in the securities case for her firm, Connaught, Marquis, and Schlaes. The clients were members of the Connaught family who had joined twenty other plaintiffs suing a broker and a securities firm for fraud. She didn't really care whether her client had lost two million. If you have fifteen million and you lose two you still have thirteen million and so what. She hadn't even begun her Christmas shopping, and she'd be in Sarasota tonight with no gifts for her parents or her sister's children.

She stamped her boots and shook the snow off her hood as she entered the building. She looked at her face in the white, enameled elevator doors. My hair is too long. I am not that innocent. Also, it's beginning to go gray. She smoothed her hair away from her face as the doors opened and brushed the snow crystals off her collar. Another vertical ride. She was always riding elevators and moving vertically. Someday she'd get on an elevator and it would move horizontally. She wouldn't . even raise her eyebrows. Once she'd known the difference between horizontal and vertical integration. It had something to do with antitrust and oligopoly.

She was alone again as the doors closed. There was something very surgical about this elevator's walls. She looked very thin. Like a thin nurse in funny coat. Why do nurses wear white? Why don't lawyers wear black robes with white pleated blouses and those funny black hats like the grinning men in the Daumier sketches or like the Nazi jurists who always wore those neat little pleated blouses? She shook her hair out and ran a comb through it. She was too thin and she'd drunk too much last night.

"My God, Julia," Ted had said to her. "I feel like I'm holding a bag of bones." "I am a bag of bones, darling," she'd answered. "We all are. We just have different coverings." What an asinine remark, just when she was looking for nurturing. If she could have, she would have slipped out of her skin and handed it to him, molted on his living room rug like a giant caterpillar, an immediate metamorphosis. She'd leave him the wind in her bones. She smiled. Where was Norman's leaf? She saw her face in the enamel doors. The fragile, white, enamel face, a perfectly made-up geisha, gray eyes, lavender lipstick. She was very, very tired. Little drops of perspiration were coming to her forehead and her legs were weak underneath the leather boots. She didn't want to go to another boring conference on another meaningless securities case. She wanted to be on a hidden beach somewhere with a straw hat over her face and the sun burning down on her breasts.

Julia wasn't surprised that the Atkinson and Lawrence conference room had electric draw drapes. When she sat down she noticed that Nicholas Barr, the associate hosting the conference, was buzzing the draw drapes slowly back and forth across the glass partition that divided the conference room from the corridor. Another kind of acting out, an unconscious opening and closing. She nodded to him. He nodded back and buzzed the drapes slowly across the partition.

She spread her damp fur coat over the back of the chair and took her box of cigarettes out. The man across from her was short with a black beard; she recognized him, Jeffrey someone. She couldn't remember his last name. He was another Atkinson and Lawrence associate. She'd remembered Nicholas and this man Jeffrey. She'd used a memory trick when they'd been introduced. Not Nicholas and Alexandra she'd told herself. Nicholas and Jeffrey. Alongside Jeffrey there was a gap of three chairs and Stephen someone taking notes and then another man she hadn't met, thin, horn-rimmed glasses, pin-striped suit, his hands folded in back of his head. At the head of the table, a blond, balding man with a British guard's mustache was talking very quietly, almost mumbling. Julia could barely hear him as she sat down. She lit a cigarette and shook her hair back over her shoulder.

The host buzzed the draw drapes closed again.

"Please, Nick," she said.

"Please what, Julia?"

"The drapes."

"Oh, I'm sorry."

"It's too early in the morning."

"Can I get you something, Julia?"

"Yes, you can get me a surrogate."

The man with the horn-rims across from her smiled and sat up. He folded his hands in a pyramid and stared at her.

The lawyer with the mustache at the head of the table kept on talking in a quiet, flat voice. "We have a deposition schedule and of course we need people to prepare for them. Now if any of you want to volunteer, okay, we can try to make up teams."

The wristwatch buzzer went off.

The blond man with the mustache looked annoyed.

Stephen looked up from his notes and pressed a button on his watch. "I can't be on a team," he said. "I'll be in Washington for three weeks starting next week. I'll do some backup but nothing original. No first seat responsibilities." He began writing again.

The blond man continued without expression. "How many of you can be on a team?"

No one raised a hand.

He didn't say anything. He just pursed his lips and

pretended to look through the glass partition although the drapes were shut.

Julia closed her eyes. All I want to do is get up and leave. She wanted to stop booking time. Empty time, time filled with absolutely nothing, time like the gray time inside a cocoon, a lacuna of time. She didn't want anything to do with teams. She'd had enough of two-somes.

"Does this have to be a project?" she suddenly said. "Why don't those people who want a particular witness depose that witness, and those who don't just stay away. We don't have to have a commission."

The host buzzed the drapes partially open.

"Nick, if you do that one more time, I'm going to leave," she told him.

"Oh, Julia, don't leave. We've just begun. It wouldn't be polite to leave."

"I'm not getting involved with a deposition over the holidays." She felt for her glasses. They were on top of her head and when she brought them down the room turned a soothing amber.

"I'm not suggesting that," the blond man said. "We're looking at thirty days from now, well into January, maybe February." He yawned and covered his mouth.

A squawk box sounded on a side table, and a voice came crackling over it. "This is Bryan Colmar here. I hope you're all making yourselves at home."

"Yes sir," Nick said to the box.

"I'm sorry I can't be there, Nick, apologize to every-one for me." Colmar was a senior trial lawyer with At-kinson and Lawrence.

"Everyone is comfortable, sir." Nick looked directly at the squawk box and fingered the control cord for the drapes.

He buzzed the drapes apart.

"I'm leaving, Nick," Julia said. "You gentlemen dispose of the deposition issue."

"Is everyone comfortable? Nick, did you send some coffee around?" the voice said from the box. "Did I hear someone say they're leaving?"

"That was counsel making a joke."

"I'm sorry, I'm probably interrupting something."

"You're not interrupting anything, sir." Nick was out of his seat and was unconsciously kneeling on one knee before the box on the table.

The man across from her tossed his pencil into the air as she left.

"Julia isn't up to the rigors of a litigation practice," she heard Nick telling the others as she walked out the door.

Back in her office, she immediately touched the plant as she entered. Norman's remark about being alone. Okay, so she was alone, divorced three years and still alone. Everyone is alone. Everyone ends up alone. She got her watering can out from the closet. The earth around the plant was cracked. Nick was even a bigger fool than Ted. He didn't even realize he was kneeling when he was talking to the box. If she could just get through the afternoon. She finished watering and sat down at her desk. For some reason she began cutting her hair over her desk. Certainly she was too innocent and she should be shorn of innocence. Everything was an acting out, wasn't it, Norman, even this cutting of the hair. How thin the air is inside a cocoon. Snip. How stultifying. Snip. She had a luncheon date with Mary, her friend who was studying to be a doctor. Mary, who sewed beautifully with her left hand; they'd made her sew with her right hand and still she'd been the only person in the class who had stitched the dog's bowel closed. The stitches of the other students had torn. She held another piece of hair. Snip. She was crying now.

"So what happens, Mary, to the dogs after you operate on them?"

"Oh, they die of course. But they're sort of like from farms in Southern Illinois and they never learned to follow the hunter and would run off and chase butterflies."

Snip. Julia K., she said to herself. Stop worrying. Stop building a psychodrama. She caught the fine strands of her hair on the papers on her desk. She had taken off two inches all the way around. Now if she could just hold the rest of herself together until she got on the plane.

There was a soft knock on her door. Claudia stood there with a fresh-faced young woman, dressed in a long woolen sweater, no cosmetics, about twenty-two, obviously a student. "Julia, this is Kimberly Bascomb; she has an appointment with you, an interview."

"I don't know anything about an interview."

"Julia, it's in your diary." Claudia looked at her.

"Sit down, Ms. Bascomb," Julia said to the young woman. Claudia shut the door.

Julia made a paper cone for the hair trimmings, like a funnel, and let them all fall into her teak wastebasket.

"Why do you want to be a lawyer, Ms.Bascomb?"

"I think I really want to help people."

"This is a bad place to help people, Ms. Bascomb. We don't help people here."

The young woman was silent.

"This firm of eighty-five men and three women is not exactly the cutting edge of the legal profession, Ms. Bascomb." Julia held her scissors up. "We help hamburger corporations and toilet paper manufacturers, but we don't help people." Julia put the scissors down.

"I would still like to apply."

"I don't think you should," Julia said quietly, "In fact, I won't permit it. Go someplace else. Go where the sun shines occasionally. You can always come back and get yourself a tailored suit and a briefcase and be an advisor to chicken franchisers."

"Ms. Kiefer, you've become a partner in this firm, that's an accomplishment."

"Is it?"

"I think it is."

"Don't be beguiled." Julia began making another paper cone. She picked up the scissors and snipped an inch of her hair and dropped the cuttings in the paper cone.

"Here, Ms. Bascomb, is a cornucopia of sorts. Take it with you. Someday, when you think about our meeting, you'll realize that I really gave you something."

THE BUTTERFLY

She sat back on the reception room couch, and, as she settled herself, her hands automatically felt for the edges of her slip along the fullness of her inner thighs where the fat lapped over the tops of her stockings. She then noticed the red chair. She was amused that a law office would have a red chair in its reception room. She had expected old colors—russets, grays—and Daumier caricatures in thin black frames, and the modular red chair of rough, striated fabric touched her with minute suspicion. She looked up at the young receptionist and tried to smile what she thought would be an appropriate widow's smile, but the girl was talking on the phone and didn't notice her. So she reached for a magazine and sat back heavily into the leather cushions and began looking through her purse for her reading glasses.

She had come downtown for the opening of her husband's safety deposit box. She knew there would be nothing of value in the box. Everything she and Walter owned was in joint tenancy: the four-flat building, their savings account, their war bonds. It would be enough with Social Security to see her through. She felt all the fuss about probate was a waste of time. She would tell the lawyers that her husband had been a very careful man, everything was "joint," and there was no need for probate. They could just fill out the tax forms, charge her a small fee, and that would be it. She had already changed over the bank accounts and collected Walter's insurance policy. She was determined to keep things simple. Walter always said, "After I'm gone, Libby will steer a straight course " Still, she had a feeling that the lawyers would confuse her and give her advice she wouldn't understand. So, as she looked through the magazine, the touch of suspicion that she had felt began to grow, and she was even more determined to be firm and cautious in dealing with her property.

Libby Martin was a widow of two weeks' mourning. Two weeks ago she had awakened, padded into the kitchen to set her coffee boiling, dressed, had her breakfast, fed the canary a fresh orange slice, and then had gone into the bedroom to wake her husband. As she pulled the bedroom curtains back she could see the fresh, newly seeded lawn, a down of green patches in the shadows of the huge oaks. The morning light was on her peonies, and from her window she watched tiny ants feeding on the sweet sap of the peony buds. When she turned to wake her husband, she saw for the first time in the same fresh light his cold, blue face and the dullness of his eyes. He was dead and had strangulated on his tongue.

As she stood over her dead husband, she extended the forefinger of her right hand and slowly reached forward and closed his eyelids. She had known at a glance. There was no need to call the rescue squad. He had died peacefully in his sleep. She plumped the pillows and, cradling his head, gently lifted it on the pillows and smoothed his hair alongside his ears. Then she went to her medicine chest and found a puff of cotton. She drenched the cotton with her favorite cologne. Returning to the bedroom she pulled the sheet over Walter and daubed the sheet in several places with the cotton. She opened each of the bedroom windows, paused at an open window to breathe the fresh garden air, then left the bedroom and closed the door. When she called the police to tell of her husband's death she began to cry for the first time. The tears came to her as though they were seeping from tiny fissures all through her body, and then, suddenly, she was screaming at the kitchen light fixture, and she covered her head with her hands and began sobbing. After that moment in the kitchen, though, she had never again really cried.

The only remnant of Walter's death that appeared cruelly upon her face was what she called her "Soutine mouth." The night before the funeral she noticed in the mirror that her mouth was swollen and misshapen. Where formerly her lips had been thin and barely noticeable, now her mouth gaped in an open circle. Her lips were purple and open. She appeared to herself like a peasant woman she had seen in a drawing by Chaim Soutine, her mouth a broad circle of paint, heavy, sagging, a hole edged by purple chalk, her lower lip hanging as if it had been pulled away from her face. She tried to close her lips, but the nerves seemed to have given away. So, for several days now, she had worn what she called her Soutine mouth and joked about it, knowing that the condition would pass, but facing the world with this visible wound through which her sadness poured. In time, she knew, when she had emptied herself of sadness, her lips would grow thin again, and the wound would close as a purple moss rose closes at nightfall.

Now, ten days after the funeral, sitting here in the lawyer's office, she felt very much alone. She had lived with Walter Martin for forty years. They had been forty precise years of careful, disciplined living. Their vacations had always been spent during the last two weeks in August at the same resort in northern Wisconsin where they'd spent their honeymoon. Then, always, the second week in January, Walter would be off to New York for the hardware convention. Walter had been a hardware buyer for a large department store in the city. On his death, the president of the company called at her home and presented her with a check for Walter's group insurance and a scroll citing Walter for his years of service. She had been civil to the man, although she couldn't get her gaping mouth to close. She apologized for what she called her cold, and, as she served tea, she kept covering her mouth with a handkerchief. Yes, the years had come too quickly, but they faced them together with caution and thrift, paying off the mortgage on their four-flat building, saving for their old age, deferring their happiness for what Walter often referred to as their "golden years." And now she was alone, sitting here in his lawyer's office, with her mouth still hanging open, wondering about the cautious, careful years that had worn from her the brightness of her youth and all her expectations. She was a widow, and her mourning, her distress, her mouth, were they really for the death of her husband or did the greater portion of the sadness flow for her own undoing?

She hesitated to think abut such things. It was better not to think. She would be kept busy. She still had her Thursday afternoons at the hospital and then, of course, the League of Women Voters and her bridge game on Fridays. These were the regular patterns of her life: the hospital, community activity, and bridge. If they were rigid patterns, it was the rigidity that would sustain her, keep her busy and unthinking. She had always been too sensitive. Walter had loved that quality in her, but he warned her against it, told her she was "day dreaming" and brought her out of it by having her do their account books or help him with his stock market activities. He didn't really play the market. It was his great hobby. He kept charts and graphs and reams of materials. He wrote to hundreds of companies for their annual reports and financial statements. Every Christmas he would treat himself to a new volume on securities and proudly put it up on his hobby shelf. Often she would urge him to withdraw some of their savings and take a chance, buy a stock that he had charted, but he always laughed at her and told her perhaps someday he would, after they had enough put away to take care of themselves. He was very regular about their savings. Each month he would add to their account. He had never let Libby draw against the savings. If she wanted some clothes or if there was a medical bill to pay, he'd see to it, but their savings were never to be touched. On interest months, he'd calculate to the penny the amount they were due and stop over at the bank on his lunch hour and have the amount stamped in the book. He loved to come home that evening and show Libby the fresh entry.

Still, the quality of dreaming never left her and all the years with Walter had not really deprived her of her ability to fantasize. It was the one luxury she allowed herself. Perhaps it was the only area of herself that she had kept from him, her dreams, her musings and what she thought of as her special moments. The moments when she would sit across from him and dream while he was working with his accounts or his charts had sustained her with an elusive brightness. Walter was dour, unbending, and parsimonious, and Libby acquired these characteristics as secondary traits in the ecology of their marriage. Yet she retained for herself a private personality that, as the years passed, still remained fresh and hopeful. At Walter's funeral in the old chapel at the cemetery she had worn her sturdy, low-heeled walking shoes when she came down the aisle before the audience of mourners. She had walked stiffly and briskly to the front row. Still, she couldn't help but notice the rose color of the sunlight that cut across the aisle through the high stained-glassed chapel window. She walked quickly through its brightness but nevertheless she felt its touch upon her as she walked. It was this quality of hers, the ability to feel special things, that she feared must now die with Walter's death. His shadow was gone and with his passing, her structure, the foundation of her life, had suddenly disappeared. That is why she was frightened and her mouth gaped open. Now she had only her own fragility to rely on and, beneath it, a few patterns of structure, her bridge games, charity, a few friends. Therefore, she hesitated to think. She only wanted to act out her life within the few familiar patterns she had built for herself. She dared not go beyond, out into her dreams, and she mourned for her lost dreams.

There were some flowers in a yellow bud vase on the receptionist's desk. She noticed the flowers and overcame an urge to pick at some of the dead blooms and tidy up the arrangement. Instead, she looked up brightly at the girl, as if her wait for the lawyer was about to come to an end. She wanted to be recognized and to get about her business. Just when she had resolved to ask the girl to ring Mr. Walston again, a tall young man came hurriedly into the reception room. Although they had never met, she knew it was her Mr. Walston and she stood up, letting her glasses fall and dangle from the chain around her neck as she introduced herself.

Walston was a tall young man dressed in a soft flannel suit. He walked ahead of her and led her into his office. There was a leather frame on his desk, divided into brass-rimmed ovals. In each oval there was a photograph of a child and, in the center, a young woman. His degrees and his license were framed on the wall and behind his desk there was a large cork canister with a metal medallion looped around it on which was engraved "Tabac." Walston leaned back in his chair and selected a pipe from a rack.

"Sorry to have kept you sitting there. We're due at the bank in ten minutes. I had a long distance phone call that I just couldn't interrupt."

"I'm anxious to get on with this, Mr. Walston," she said. "I hate formality. I just want to sign the necessary papers and be on my way."

She liked the intense look of the young man. He looked at her directly when he spoke and he had a smile that made his face come alive quickly. She liked intensity in young people. She would be pleased to let his energy work for her, get all this concluded. God knew she didn't have the energy for it.

"I only met your husband a few times," Walston said. "He was Mr. Harrington's client, but, when Mr. Harrington took ill, I was called in to revise your husband's will."

"I know. He often spoke of you. I know he liked you. I think the two of you would have become very good friends."

"I'm very sorry, Mrs. Martin. I would have liked to have known him better."

Walston handed her a form. "Here's a copy of the application for inheritance tax consents, and here's a consent letter from the Attorney General's office."

"Do we need his consent to open the box?" she asked.

The young man tapped his pipe on his ashtray and smiled. "Well, the state wants to make certain there'll be sufficient assets to pay the inheritance tax before they'll release anything to you. Don't worry. They'll have their box examiner there to take an inventory. They'll know what's there from his listing. The box examiner lists all the contents, gives the bank one copy, gives us another, and files another with the inheritance tax office."

"I'm not so certain I approve of that," she said. "Having this man looking over everything. Anyway, there'll be nothing to list. Maybe old photographs, letters, and I think our birth certificates. I don't think I've been near that vault for twenty years. It was really my husband's box."

"Did you bring the key?" Walston said.

"Good God, no," she gasped. "I didn't even stop to think."

"We'll have it drilled open," Walston said.

"I've been so rattle-brained. Anyway, Walter kept the key at his office."

"Don't worry. People forget; happens all the time. I'll call the bank and they'll have a locksmith come down and drill it open." He reached for the phone and gave instructions to his secretary.

"I'm perfectly stupid," Libby said, feeling embarrassed as she stood up. "I never gave a thought to the key."

They left his office and he brought her coat from the reception room. Then they took the elevator down to the street. The elevator stopped halfway down and a little man got on and began to stare at Libby. He was an elderly man, shabbily dressed, with a heavy garlic breath that Libby immediately sensed. The man wore bifocals that enlarged his eyes. Libby quickly looked away from the eyes, knowing that this man was ill, a pathetic, misshapen gnome. She held her coat bunched up in her arm close to her nose so the fragrance from her fur collar would be near. When she and Walston left the elevator the man turned the other way. She was relieved to be out in the street away from him. The fresh air felt good and the young lawyer was very solicitous as they crossed the street, taking her arm and protecting her against the traffic. Still she had a prescience about the old man, as if he were a harbinger of age and illness awaiting her.

The bank was only two blocks away and they soon arrived and walked down the deep stone stairs to the vault section. She was careful going down the stairway with her heels. She felt that if she slipped she might keep falling into this cavern below the city streets, to be sealed off forever by the men in gray uniforms standing behind the huge vault door. The door was made of glass and steel like a mammoth open sarcophagus, cog wheels and gears exposed behind glass.

As they entered the vault, the chief guard came

over to them and led them into another room where a locksmith was already waiting, electric drill in hand. A man with a briefcase was also standing there, the box examiner from the Attorney General's office. As soon as she was introduced as the widow, the locksmith climbed a small foot ladder to the box and started drilling the locks open. The whine of the drill was the only noise in the room. The locksmith made two neat little holes and the metal shavings from his bores flew in the light like silver pollen.

The whining of the drill ended and the locksmith flipped open the door to the box and looked down at the guard.

"Come down off the ladder and I'll get the tin," the guard said. The guard, a heavy man, took careful steps up the ladder and reached in and pulled out the long slim black box. Then the guard, the box examiner, and Walston led Libby into another room, and they all sat at a large conference table with the box square in the middle of the table. The guard handed around a clipboard and asked them all to sign as being present and told them they were not to leave the room without signing again. Then he left, and the box examiner asked her to open the box.

Libby pulled the box toward her and opened it. A few papers were lying loose on top of several bulky envelopes, and she selected one and removed it from the box.

"Here's our marriage license," she said. "It was sweet of Walter to have kept it all these years," she said quietly. She placed the paper neatly in front of her and reached into the box again.

"And here's his discharge paper from the Army. He

was a soldier in the First War, you know," she said proudly, her eyes glistening. She placed the document in front of her.

"This must be his birth certificate," she said. She removed the certificate and placed it on the pile.

"That document with the blue cover," Walston said. "May I have it?" Libby handed the paper to the lawyer.

"It's the original will, Mrs. Martin," the lawyer said. "It's the same as the copy that I mailed to you. I'll take this and file it with the Probate Clerk."

"I assume the wife is the principal beneficiary," the box examiner said.

"You assume right," Walston said. "The only beneficiary. There were no children."

Libby watched the box examiner for a sign of approbation, but the man was writing notes on a long yellow sheet and didn't look up at her. "All right, let's get on with it," he said as he made his notes. "I have another examination in an hour."

"I'm sorry," she said. "I seem to be going at this very slowly. I had no idea that there would be so many papers here."

"You should have scheduled this for more than an hour," the box examiner said rather curtly to Walston. "Why don't you have the lady here look over the personal items, and you and I can go through those large envelopes. Maybe we can save time that way."

"Go right ahead, gentlemen," Libby said. "I'm sure you won't find anything of value, just old family records. My husband saved everything, you know." She took the loose papers remaining in the box and began to go through them. A little transparent envelope fell from the papers. It contained a butterfly specimen. "It's a lovely specimen," Libby said, holding the envelope up to the light. "Walter was also a lepidopterist. I know nothing about his collection, but this must be a peculiarly fine specimen if he kept it locked up in his vault."

"He was also a collector of stock certificates," the box examiner said. He removed the contents from one of the large envelopes and spread several certificates on the table.

"Walter was a great hobbyist," Libby said, looking at the certificates. She felt her throat growing tight and her hand trembled slightly as she picked up one of the certificates. "He played the market as a hobby . . . as an avocation. He never bought anything. He kept graphs and charts but he never owned a share of stock in his life. I'm sure they're not real."

Mr. Walston opened another of the large envelopes and removed a sheaf of stock certificates.

The box examiner stood up and looked at the documents. "Of course they're real. There's small fortune in just these two envelopes. You must be kidding, lady."

"I cannot believe you," Libby said emphatically.

"It's true," the box examiner said, opening two more envelopes and removing more stock certificates. "You mean your husband never told you about this, lady? Why, this is as fine a portfolio of blue chips as I've ever listed. There must be over a million bucks here."

"Mr. Walston, tell me what this man is saying," Libby gasped.

"He's saying that you're a very wealthy woman, Mrs. Martin. The certificates are genuine. I'm just as surprised as you are. Your husband never mentioned a word of this to me."

"You are telling me the truth, Mr. Walston?"

"Mrs. Martin, I would have no reason to tilt windmills with you."

"Lady, for God's sake," the box examiner said, opening the remainder of the envelopes and spreading bundles of certificates before her. "Look at this list: General Motors, IBM, Pure Oil, Reynolds Tobacco, Xerox, Commonwealth Edison . . . do you know what this is? For God's sake, lady, it's a fortune."

Libby reached out again for one of the certificates. Her hand moved across the table slowly, as a wounded animal crawls to tall grass for shelter. She brought the certificate up before her and looked at it carefully. "The Pure Oil Company," she said. "This is a certificate for one hundred shares of the common stock of The Pure Oil Company," she said slowly. Then she looked at the men incredulously.

"There's more than a million here," the box examiner said.

"But we were very ordinary people. Saving for our old age. We saved for years. Paid off the mortgage on our four flat. I have our savings account . . . Walter's insurance."

"It's all yours, lady." the box examiner said. "Ask your counselor here. He's got the will."

"We were saving for our golden years. Walter called them our golden years. We were going to buy a little home together. Do some traveling. We never went anywhere. Never saw anything. We never lived . . . we were waiting." She began to cry. She hadn't cried since the day of Walter's death. "Always waiting . . . what were we waiting for?" she asked tearfully and covered her face with her hands.

Mr. Walston got up and left the room to get her a glass of water. The box examiner began to stack the securities in piles. Then Walston returned and gave her the water and excused himself. He sat down with the box examiner and they began to divide the securities. As she drank the water, she could hear the lawyer calling off the certificate numbers to the box examiner. The voice of the lawyer sounded like a liturgical chant, and Libby felt like a little girl hidden far back in the church listening to the canticle of a priest.

As she sat watching the men counting her husband's secret wealth, she tried to reach for a fantasy, a dream that would explain this to her. She felt the fantasy coming as she picked up the little glassine package that held the butterfly specimen. She held the transparent envelope up to the light. Then she thought of herself as the butterfly, trapped in a jar, her husband holding the jar and cruelly watching her futile wing beats as she fell to the bottom leaving a pattern of wing dust along the edges of the glass. The fantasy brought her no comfort. She was the butterfly in the envelope. And Walter Martin had trapped her in her youth and locked her in his vault. She looked at the butterfly against the light, its patterns like an x-ray film slapped on a viewer, all the color gone, sere and delicate, the edges of its wings broken and serrated.

If this was not all a joke, a fantastic, contrived hoax, if she was really a rich woman, the owner of this hoard of stock, well then she could take an ocean voyage. Why not? It would be her first gift to herself in forty years. The ocean air along her face might give her clarity and freshness. She dropped the envelope containing the butterfly in her purse. She would take the specimen to the Orient and in Hong Kong have it modeled into a pendant, gold latticework edged with jade and pearls. She would have an artisan reconstruct its beauty. It could be worn on a thin chain from her neck as she traveled, a magnificent piece of jewelry. Then later, on the return voyage, watching the waves break, long and white and violent, the butterfly hanging lightly from her neck, she would sip hot bouillon and think again about what her husband had done to her.

PICASSO IS DEAD

Sylvan Kalisher is standing at the edge of the motel pool in his straw sun hat and new terry cloth beach robe. The Kalisher family has come to Sanibel Island on the Gulf Coast off Fort Myers for a two-week vacation in early April, during the spring school recess.

Sylvan is a lawyer in Chicago and an amateur litterateur. On weekends, he writes short stories and then sends them off in flat brown envelopes to college literary quarterlies. So far he is unpublished, but he treasures the coy little notes he receives from student editors, and, after ninety-six submissions, he has already received one conditional acceptance from the University of Alaska for a story centered on onanism. *Chicago Review* had previously rejected the same piece as " . . . a nice story, but too nice."

As Sylvan stands at the edge of the pool, he tentatively thrusts his right big toe into the water and muses about the note from *Chicago Review*. He wonders what they meant by " . . . nice but too nice." He's still wounded by the round, looping, feminine handwriting with circles as 'i' dots. The dots have lodged in his psyche. He knows the note was probably written by an eighteen-year-old in denim flares and pigtails, maybe a Maoist looking for revolutionary consciousness in a story about onanism. But still it bothers him.

The people from Juneau had replied with a concise, neat, typewritten note: "We like the story . . . the theme of a transvestite as abbot of an inner city monastery hangs true . . . overtones of Thomas Merton . . . like to publish it . . . budget permitting . . . perhaps a year or more . . . may we keep it?"

Sylvan immediately shot off a check to Alaska and subscribed, and told them by all means keep the story " . . . only for God's sake publish it." He's never heard from them. Each quarter, though, he receives a copy of the review (the last issue devoted to Eskimo Concrete Poetry and the official Sitka archives of Eskimo folk music and lute songs).

Sylvan shakes his head and puts his toe in the water again. He slowly removes his beach robe. Then he removes his hat. His wife, Baby Kalisher, is sitting at the pool greasing their three year old, Joel, with Sea & Ski.

"Match me, Dahdee," Joel is saying. Watch me.

Sylvan looks at the child with interest. The little boy is dressed in an orange kapok life jacket, a diver's mask, and snorkel tube and flippers. Joel has never been swimming before. His first venture to the kiddie stairs at the far end of the pool will be presided over by Sylvan, who has been instructed by his wife, "Dive in and help Joel, Sylvan. Can't you see he's waiting? Dive, already."

Sylvan dives. As he hits the cold water, he knows he should be anticipating its smooth feeling, but all he can focus on as he goes down is his wife's remark when he led Joel out to her for the Sea & Ski rubdown. Baby Kalisher had looked up at him from the chaise lounge, her lavender glasses down on her nose and her paperback on her flat stomach. "Tallulah Bankhead was a lesbian," she said, as she held her arms out to Joel, "Come mommy . . . a bisexual."

As Sylvan does the breaststroke to the kiddie stairs, he thinks about the remark, and then he feels a slight heart twinge, a spasm in his side, and he stops stroking and begins to float. He opens his eyes below the water. Children's legs sweep past him in blue underwater tag games. The spasm frightens him. Ted Roethke had died in a pool. Where? In Seattle? He remembers Allan Seager's biography, the description of Roethke's death—a plunge into the pool and then Roethke dead. My God, Sylvan thinks. He floats face downward toward Joel, the pain still flickering.

As Sylvan comes up from the water, his son stands looking down at him from behind the diver's mask.

"Hi, Joel," Sylvan says cheerily. The pain is gone now.

"Me not Joel. Me Georgie."

"Hi, Georgie."

"Me not Georgie."

"Who are you, baby? You're Joel."

"Me Chidis."

"Chidis?"

"Yah, me Chidis."

Sylvan stands in the shallow water and holds his arms out as the child hesitantly backs down the kiddie stairs. Joel is reciting "Ring Around the Rosy" in a lisping baby falsetto. When he reaches "ashes, ashes, all fall down," he sticks his little rump in the water and then climbs back up the stairs. He is a precocious child, and Sylvan isn't worried about Joel's imaginary friends.

"Now Georgie come down," Joel says, still chanting the verse in his false voice. He carefully immerses his rear in the water at the bottom of the stairs, then struggles up again, flapping in his fins like a baby platypus. "Now Chidis turn. Chidis come down." Joel sings until he reaches "ashes, ashes," and does his dip.

"Chidis is a big boy diver," Sylvan says to the child, and, giving him a reassuring pat, he sends him up the stairs.

Baby Kalisher, though, is frantic about the child's imaginary friends. She's even beginning to talk about sending Joel to a psychiatrist. The other morning at breakfast she looked up at Sylvan, her spoon holding a piece of papaya in mid-air, and said, "Do you think Dr. Levine would see Joel? I know they take them at four . . . but at three? Maybe just an exploratory session—an evaluation."

"Forget it," Sylvan had said.

"No, I'm serious. This business with the imaginary friends."

"It's a thing with three year olds. The kid will outgrow it."

Baby popped the piece of melon into her mouth and daintily spit some seeds into her paper napkin.

"It drives me crazy, Syl . . . Chidis and Georgie, Chidis and Georgie. . . . He's such a bright child. But I think he's overcompensating, hallucinating. And at three he should already be toilet-trained. I try. God knows I try."

As Sylvan stands in the bright sun that beats down on him through the palm trees, he has a vision of Dr. Levine's office, the sleek Danish teak furniture and the Miró prints. He went through two years of Levine with his daughter, Katrinka. He can already see the monthly statement, "Professional Services, Joel—3 visits—$105." Levine's looping handwriting reminds him of the *Chicago Review* editor's handwriting. Levine is a pompous ass. Sylvan would like to take an ax to his goddamn teak desk and tell him where to shove his statements with the handwritten "Professional Services."

Suddenly, Sylvan remembers a flash of Salinger. One of Salinger's children had an imaginary friend. Was it the little girl in "A Perfect Day for Bananafish"? Or the child in "Uncle Wiggily in Connecticut"? Was there a child in "Wiggily"? The sun beats on Sylvan's bald spot, and he fights through the heat to try to recall his Salinger. The man on the beach—who was it, Seymour Glass? That's it, Seymour and the little girl. Of course it was Seymour, or maybe Marvin, Marvin Glass? No, that's a man in the toy business in Chicago. Or was it the other story, "Uncle Wiggily"—a child in bed, reciting to an imaginary friend? God, how he wished he could remember his Salinger. He'd look it up when they got back to Chicago. It was "Bananafish," the child in "Bananafish," and Seymour committed suicide. Shot himself. Did he shoot himself? He can remember the wife talking to her mother on the phone, the hotel room in Miami, the wife painting her toenails and talking about Seymour to her mother. How could she paint her toenails and talk on the phone at the same time?

"Sylvan. You're not *watching* that child." Baby Kalisher's sharp voice comes crackling across from the pool apron.

"You're not matching," Joel says, mimicking his mother.

"Sylvan. Can't I have my moment?" Baby demands, looking up from the Tallulah paperback. "Can't *you* be responsible?"

"Chidis is matching me," Joel says.

"It's too goddamn hot," Sylvan answers. "Throw me the Block Out; I'll rub some on the top of my head and make myself responsible."

"You should be wearing your hat, Syl," Baby says as she reaches over the chaise lounge and throws the tube of sun oil. "And don't be so antagonistic."

"All right," Sylvan answers her. "Stop screaming, already. I thought you left that condescending voice back in the suburbs."

Fortunately, no other adults were present and the two Kalishers could speak freely.

"Rub some on Joel, too," Baby was calling. "Rub it good on his little back."

Sylvan takes the oil and spreads it on his bald spot. Then he presses his palm with the oil between Joel's shoulder blades. He can feel the child's rib cage and the thin fluttering of Joel's heartbeat. It gives him a sense of the child's fragility, and at the same time a feeling of awe, the child's heartbeats transmitting to the father through the palm of his hand a fragile sense of union, the mystery of the relation of child to father. Sylvan rubs the oil gently.

It is almost noon. The sun is now directly overhead, a white ball through the palm fronds. The Kalisher daughter, Katrinka Kalisher, age nine, suddenly appears at the edge of the pool and bends over to consult with Sylvan. She looks perturbed.

"Daddy," she says in an excited vioce, "can I be Unitarian today, instead of Jewish?"

Sylvan would like to clap himself on the forehead to accent his exasperation at the remark, but the act of dragging his hand up through the water to clap his head would be too trying in the heat.

"What are you, a vaudevillian?" he says churlishly to the little girl. Joel meanwhile is aiming his bottom at Daddy. "Ashes, ashes," he sings happily, and floats out to Sylvan.

"No, a Unitarian," Katrinka responds dramatic-ally and stamps her foot. "Momma's a Unitarian," she hisses at Sylvan, glancing darkly at Baby Kalisher prone in the sun. "And so is Tiffany." Katrinka tosses her head in the direction of the parasol table, and Sylvan sees the shadow of a young girl standing with her arms folded under the umbrella.

"Tiffany who?" he says, as if he didn't know already.

"Tiffany my new friend. She's a Unitarian and she lives in Ohio. She's never heard of Jewish."

"Okay. So go with Tiffany. Go."

"It's all right, Daddy?" Katrinka says, smiling.

"Don't bother me," Sylvan says, acquiescing in the heat.

The two little girls go off hand in hand, their long hair flailing behind them in the sea breeze. Soon they are clacking shuffleboard discs on the court hidden under the trees.

Sylvan decides to take Joel for a walk on the beach.

"Come, Joel," he says, and leads the child up the kiddie stairs and around the pool, to where Baby is lying, half sleeping. He picks up a long sliver of palm frond and flicks his wife on her stomach.

"Joel and I are going shelling." She is startled, and squints as she sits up and automatically reaches for a cigarette. "Put a shirt on him, the blue one with the long sleeves," she says.

"Katrinka is being Unitarian with Tiffany," Sylvan answers. "They're playing shuffleboard. Tiffany is from Ohio where there aren't any Jewish." Sylvan is being informative.

"So let them have fun," Baby says as she tugs the shirt over Joel and hugs him. "Momma loves her baby boy."

"Tiffany is a great name," Sylvan says. "I suppose she has a sister named Kimberly."

"So—Tiffany, Kimberly—big deal, Syl."

"Okay. Come on, Joel. Come with Daddy."

"Me Chidis," Joel says impishly, then waddles off in the direction of the beach.

As Sylvan and Joel pass the shuffleboard court, Katrinka ignores them and pretends to be fiercely concentrating on her game. Sylvan takes a good look at Tiffany. She's a fat little girl in a halter and a peaked, red polka-dot sun hat. As she shoots her disc, she jumps up and down and then immediately runs downcourt, her sandals clapping, to check her position on the scoring triangle.

"I beat," she is screaming at Katrinka. Triumph is smeared on her red cheeks as Katrinka now sends her disc down the court, knocking Tiffany's disc aside.

"No, you don't," Katrinka screams joyously as she runs down the court. "I won you. I won you. Didn't I, Daddy?" she suddenly demands of Sylvan as he passes.

"You beat her," Sylvan says carefully. Tiffany looks at him with scorn, like a customs officer inspecting an old immigrant, but she remains silent, and Sylvan and Joel plod on to the rim of the sea.

Joel is frightened by the sound of the waves, and he holds his father's hand, but then he notices the birds.

"Birdies," he says, pointing, and runs along the shore to chase the sandpipers and gulls. The sandpipers move ahead of him, keeping just out of reach, like toy wind-up birds strutting on pavement, and the gulls whoosh over Joel's head and cackle to each other. Sylvan follows his son and carries the baby away from the birds to a cane windbreak in front of the motel, where the chairs are set up out of the wind.

Sylvan sits and Joel begins to play with a large stick. There is an abandoned green kite under a chair and a spool of string. Sylvan picks up the kite and sees that the cross strut is broken. Someone had tried to repair it with a Band-aid. But as Sylvan holds the kite up to the wind, the strut caves in and the kite flutters and collapses. He begins to work on the kite, using a small piece of wood to brace the strut. He ties the brace on with string from the spool, and cuts the string with a shell edge.

As he works, he occasionally looks up to nod at the people who pass the windbreak. They're mostly pairs of matrons, in modest, old-fashioned swimsuits, who walk the beach to collect shells. They smile as they pass and see the father working with the kite and the little boy playing with his stick. A few families come by, the men sniffing the sea air, the mothers and daughters energetically stooping for shells and collecting them in plastic bags provided by the motels. A jogger runs along, followed by his dog chasing through the surf and snapping at birds. Sylvan is content to sit and work with the kite.

When the kite is ready, Sylvan stands up and holds it to the wind again.

"Now watch Daddy fly," he says to Joel.

Sylvan tests the wind and lets the kite go. It catches the air momentarily and is pulled up. Then it dives down, and Sylvan jerks it up and begins unreeling and running furiously. As he pumps down the beach, the kite gracefully takes to the air, but Sylvan feels another spasm prick his side, and he immediately stops running. The kite dumps into the sea. My God, Sylvan wonders, am I going to die on this beach? He tries to think of a writer who died flying his kite on a beach. He can't think of one. As he rests, the spasm diminishes, and he tries to pull the kite out of the water but the string breaks. He has unreeled most of the string on the beach, and he begins reeling back, retracing his steps. He can see Joel crying in front of the windbreak, and he hears the baby's howl in the wind.

"Daddy's coming back." He cups his hands and calls to Joel. "Wait there, Joel." Sylvan is still panting from the run as he reels and reels the loops of string, following the erratic pattern of his run until he finally returns to the child.

"Daddy fly away," Joel says.

"Daddy didn't fly away, Joel. Daddy only trying to fly the kite."

Sylvan calms the child and they walk along the shore leading to the front of the motel. Then Sylvan pats Joel and sends him back up to the shuffleboard court where Katrinka is still playing.

When the child leaves, Sylvan begins to walk along the shore again and heads away from the motel. He looks for the green kite on the water but the sea has already taken it, and Sylvan stuffs the reel of string in his pocket.

As he walks, he picks up a long stick and uses it to turn over shells. He sees a glob of sea ooze and pokes it with his stick and watches the way the glob moves as he pokes it. My God—that has life. He's surprised at the movement of the gel. I'll be dead on this God-forsaken beach and that thing will still be alive. He pokes it again. For some reason, the glob seems to grow smaller, sucking into itself as Sylvan prods it.

Sylvan is reminded of his wad of traveler's checks. When he arrived on the island, the wad of checks was big and fat. Every morning he inspects his coat pocket to see if the checks are still there. Each morning, though, the packet has grown slimmer. He wonders if the maids are stealing them. He envisions a hand reaching through the bedroom door with the broken lock and plucking the checks, leaving the Kalishers stranded forever on Sanibel.

Those traveler's checks are his umbilical cord to civilization, and they are *shrinking* like the mass of protoplasmic gel oozing and shrinking at his feet. Maybe he should go back to the room and see if the packet is still in his coat? And the Hertz car keys? What if he lost the keys? Joel always plays with keys. What if the kid takes the keys and drops them on the beach?

Sylvan knows he's being paranoid, but he's depressed. The brightness of the sun on the water, the heaving yellow waves and the wild fury of the surf as it comes at him depress him. And Picasso is dead. Someone at the motel told him, and Baby heard it on the news. Picasso dead at ninety-one.

Sylvan had always dreamed of himself as a spry oc-

togenarian, still writing blockbuster novels in his eight-
ies, maybe at a villa on the Riviera, taking long walks in
the evenings, occasionally bumping into Picasso. They
would exchange pleasantries along the curving stone
wall that divided their adjacent orchards. "Hello,
Maître, bon soir," he would say to his friend Picasso,
and the old man would reply, "*Ah, comment ça va,
Kalisher?*" Sylvan would answer evenly, "*Tout va
bien*," and Picasso would smile and hold his hand up,
signaling to Sylvan with looped index finger and thumb,
and they would walk together, lost in serious discussion,
down the orchard road.

Now no more conversations with Picasso. Picasso is
dead and Sylvan has lost his friend and neighbor. He
begins to wonder if, after all, he, Sylvan, will become
"Maître," will ever write that blockbuster novel he
promised himself. The one with the movie sale like
Harold Robbins's or Irving Wallace's. That would show
Chicago Review. A Sylvan Kalisher blockbuster with a
Cynthia Ozick review in the *New Republic*.

He smacks his dry lips in anticipation of Ozick's
praise and licks the salt away as he watches a formation
of pelicans eddy in along the shore and disappear
around the bend toward the Old Lighthouse. Then he
returns to the motel and walks up the steps into the cottage and, ignoring everyone, goes into his room for a
nap.

When he awakens, it's dark outside and the cottage
is empty. There's a note pasted with Scotch tape on the
TV, advising that the family has gone for stone crab and
that they'll bring some back. He goes to the refrigerator
and snaps open a beer. It's late, almost nine, and he
wonders if they went to the Laundromat after dinner.

Then he hears a car crunching on the motel drive, and Baby and the children come laughing up the stairs.

"I was beginning to worry," Sylvan says.

"You were sound asleep," Baby answers. "So we let you sleep, Syl. But we brought stone crab and mayonnaise."

"I'm starving."

"Were you *flying* a kite?" Katrinka asks incredulously. "I thought I saw you."

"I almost got it up," Sylvan says. "Then it pooped out on me."

"Fly it for me tomorrow," Katrinka asks.

"I lost it at sea, baby," Sylvan says, wiping the mayonnaise off his chin.

As he eats, he overcomes the impulse to go to the closet again to feel for his wad of traveler's checks. He wonders how Baby paid for the dinner. Maybe she used her Bankamericard. Oh, the hell with it, he thinks, and enjoys the stone crabs and beer.

The family watches TV, and then Joel is put to bed.

"Goodnight, baby," Sylvan says, as he bends over to kiss his little boy. The child kicks under his blanket and squeals at Sylvan, and sucks on his bottle in long, satisfied draughts as Sylvan brushes the tiny face with a kiss.

Then Katrinka undresses and begins to read in bed. Suddenly she calls out to her parents: "How many light-years to the moon?"

"How many what?" Baby asks.

"Light-years."

"Ask your father," Baby says.

"Too many," Sylvan answers.

"No, seriously." Katrinka is sitting up. "I'm reading about the moon and they have this problem."

"Good night," Sylvan says, and the girl pouts and then returns to her book. But, in a few moments, she is asleep with the book open on her blanket.

Baby and Sylvan are alone. Sylvan pops open two more beers and hands one to his wife. They sit together and watch TV.

"I had a pain in my side when I was swimming," Sylvan says quietly. "A sharp pain."

Baby's face is set in an anticipatory smile for humorous TV watching, a smile that's almost a mask, as if she had quickly slipped into a veil of newly acquired happiness. Sylvan can't break through to her.

"And another pain when I ran with the kite," he muttters. "Almost as bad."

Baby nods.

Sylvan can't reach her, and, as he sips his beer, he dreams of himself as bleached carrion in the sun on the beach, like the bleached bones he has seen: whale bones, porpoise bones, he doesn't know. The gulls peck at his carrion, and then the sandpipers come with their toy bird steps, a whole phalanx of sandpipers, and finally the pelicans. As each bird pecks, it comes away with a dollar bill. Sylvan's carrion is not just bleached bone; Sylvan is covered with a veil of dollar bills, a currency epidermis. As Baby is protected by her veil of TV happiness, Sylvan is protected by his parasol of currency. Only the birds are pecking away at him, tearing the dollars off one by one and stripping him to bone, leaving him on the beach, bone white in the hot light.

Sylvan shakes his head. He goes to his duffel bag

and finds a flashlight. Then he takes another beer and speaks to his wife.

"Take a walk with me."

He opens the front door and flicks his flashlight on at the palm trees. He can see the moon and the brightness of the stars. "Come on, Babe, let's take a little walk."

"You go, Syl. The Carson show is coming on."

"Please come with me."

"No, go. It's too cold."

Sylvan heads again to the rim of the sea. The tide is out, and he can see people shelling out on the flats, their flashlights tiny white dots in the darkness. He shines his light ahead of him as he walks. The tide has left the ocean floor in front of the motel, and Sylvan notices how the ocean is terraced, crenellated, the undulations of the floor revealed in the sweep of his light. He sees a chain of seaweed shaped like coils of vertebrae. The life revealed to him on the ocean floor is amazing: live cockle shells in clumps, piles of shells of all description. He tries to remember the shells he knows: jingle, cat's-eye, murex, cockle, cat's-paw, angel wing. He bends to a cluster of dead shells washed on the shore and lets them fall through his fingers.

As he recites the shell names, he is reminded of the character in an Allan Seager story who, after having been declared incompetent, is on his way by train to the hospital where he is to surrender himself for treatment. He sits alone in the train compartment and recites the names of the Channel Islands, as a litany to himself to assure his sanity. "Jersey, Guernsey, Alderney, and Sark." Sylvan thinks of the Seager story and continues

his recitation. "Murex, buttercup, cockle, and whelk."
Sylvan is sane. He stoops over and picks up a cat's-eye
and holds it to his light. It looks like a snail with an eye
of a cat. It's glistening from the sea.

Why Seager? No one ever heard of him. Seager was
Sylvan's professor at Michigan, and Seager is dead and
out of print. But Seager was good. Sylvan drops the
cat's-eye and rummages through the shell pile in front
of him and picks up a huge cockle shell. It's brown and
ugly in the light, and it's alive with pink tendrils waving
out from its shell.

He inspects the cockle shell. As he looks at the ugly
shell, he thinks of Seager, big and aristocratic with the
fine intelligence—"Jersey, Guernsey, Alderney, and
Sark." Sylvan tosses the cockle shell out to the sea. It
lands with a loud thunk and its fragile shell breaks as it
hits the flat.

To hell with *Chicago Review*.

Picasso is dead. Seager is dead. And Kalisher is
dying—with already, at forty-five, a pain in his side.
"And Kalisher is dying." A good line though. Ted
Roethke dead, too. Salinger hiding somewhere in the
woods. So who's left? Vonnegut, maybe. Cynthia Ozick
likes Vonnegut, says he is with the *zeitgeist*. Barthelme
maybe. Sylvan admires the word, *zeitgeist*. Maybe
Ozick would say he, Kalisher, is with the *zeitgeist*.

"Jersey, Guernsey, Alderney, and Sark."

"Chidis, Georgie, and the *zeigteist*."

And then Sylvan's flashlight swoops down on a perfect pair of hinged angel wing shells. They're buried in
the sea floor. He gently removes the delicate shells and
washes the sand off them. They are beautiful in the
light, white and gleaming. It's very difficult to find an

unbroken pair of angel wings, and Sylvan has found a perfect hinged pair. He's delighted. He heads back to the motel, careful to keep his tennis shoes dry as he steps over the tidal pools on the shell flats. The angel wings are safe in his pocket.

When he enters the cottage, he sees that Baby has gone to bed. The only light is at the breakfast bar where she has set the table. Sylvan undresses, but before he sleeps, he leaves the pair of angel wings with the silverware beside Baby's papaya bowl.

As he slides into bed, he feels his wife alongside him, and, as he turns to kiss her good night, another sharp pain comes to his chest. He winces and falls back on the pillow. He waits. The pain subsides. "Are you sleeping? Babe, are you sleeping?" She doesn't answer. Sylvan turns away from her and tries to calm himself into sleep. "Jersey, Guernsey, Alderney, and Sark; Jersey, Guernsey, Alderney, and Sark . . . " The sea wind blows through the window, and palm leaf shadows, cast in the silver light of the moon, flutter up and down along the bedroom wall. Coconuts clack against each other in the wind. "Jersey, Guernsey, Alderney, and Sark." His eyes are wide with terror in the silver light. The wind rushes again, and the palm shadows sway along the wall, and again the coconuts crack against each other. "Jersey, Guernsey, Alderney, and Sark."

PROFESSOR STRAUSS'S GIFT

He was sitting in a sidewalk cafe in the warm fall afternoon sunlight on a mall in downtown Chicago. He was a law professor and he had just come from the dentist. His Conflicts lecture was at two so he had stopped at the cafe for a cup of coffee before returning to the law school. His mouth still hurt. At 40 he was beginning a life of repeated dentistry, and today, when the spiral-shaped root canal files twirled deep into his canals, he had the sensation that his teeth were really being filled with tiny ancient legal scrolls, tiny replicas of Torah scrolls. The scrolls were pushed into his root canals so deeply that the language was washing into his bloodstream. Was he being infiltrated by platelets of floating Hebrew letters? Or platelets of Sumerian? In a sense, he was becoming an aging keeper of the law. He was really no different from some aging Torah teacher or ancient scribe. He looked at his fingers with a few fine blonde hairs glistening. His hand shook slightly. He had been drinking too much. He'd been alone too much.

There was a rather attractive waitress standing in the sunlight at the warming plates by the entrance to the cafe. Could a gentleman with Sumerian platelets floating in his bloodstream ask for a quiet refill of coffee? It would be an innocent request. She was paid to give coffee refills, and he wouldn't be exceeding propriety by asking her for one. Instead of Torah scrolls, he could have been infiltrated by tiny replicas of the Code of Hammurabi. He could have scrolls of the Code of Hammurabi twisted so deeply into his canals that platelets of Babylonian hieroglyphics, broad-billed platypuses, and scarabs would already be swimming inside of him (he consulted the date on his watch and looked over at the waitress).

She came to his table when she saw him staring at her.

"May I have some coffee again?"

"Yes, of course."

She was tall, slender, with high cheekbones and glasses, quite fair, and her face was tanned from the sun. She had a foreign accent and brown hair cut short. She must be about 27 or 28, he thought, perhaps German.

"Are you from Germany?"

"Germany? No," she answered with a cultured accent.

He watched her fingers as she poured the coffee, long, tapered, beautiful fingers. She wore an unusual ring, a black signet ring.

"You're wearing an interesting ring. Where are you from?"

"Poland." She pronounced it Po-land.

"Is that ring the crest of the Radziwills?"

She laughed. "No, I am not a Radziwill." She turned away from him toward another customer and then stopped and walked back to him. "Do you know about Polish nobility? I have never met an American who knows about Polish nobility."

He lifted his cup to her.

She was quite attractive, and she spoke with the manner of an educated woman. Her accent was almost English. After a few moments she returned to his table with a pot of coffee.

"Want some more?" she asked, almost jauntily.

"Do you know Kafka?" He put his hand over his cup.

"Kafka? Not too well. He is very complicated."

"You don't like him?"

"He is too morose. Is that correct, 'morose'?"

"Yes, morose is correct."

"Do you want more coffee?"

"No, no thank you."

She turned and went back to her station. "If you want some more, just notify me."

She was right, of course. Kafka was much too morose. Should he notify her? Lately he seemed to be always missing connections with women. He wasn't really seeing anyone. He dated occasionally, but he spent most evenings alone working in his office. He was trying to write a casebook on international law. He'd been put under contract by one of the large legal publishing companies. This summer he'd flown to Geneva and also spent a casual month at the United Nations in New York. All he could say for it was that it had been a good jogging summer. The summer of 1981. He'd run in Geneva, Paris, and Manhattan. But he'd spent the summer without any human connections. He knew no one who liked to touch him or hold him and he knew no one he could touch or hold.

He was practically the only customer now and she walked back to his table.

"Would you care for more?" she asked again.

"No, thank you, I've had enough."

"Very well then." She began to turn away.

"What is your name?" he said to her.

"My name?"

"Yes."

"My name is Maria."

"That's a lovely name."

"Thank you. Thank you very much." She was very formal and correct and his questioning apparently was embarrassing her.

"My name is Paul," he said.

She extended her hand. "How do you do, Paul?" she said to him with the English accent.

He smiled at her. "Where in Poland are you from?"

"From Krakow."

"Krakow. That is a beautiful city."

She wore large glasses. They made her look quite scholarly and she pushed them back on her nose and smiled. "You know Krakow?" she said, looking at him from behind the large glasses.

"No, I don't. I know it's a very old city."

"The Pope is from Krakow."

"Oh, yes."

"Would you care for a biscuit?" she asked. "If you would like, I believe there is one fresh biscuit."

"No, no thank you."

They both watched a young black man bending over a pigeon that was standing in front of a bus. The bus was about to start up and run over the pigeon. The man very gently put his hands over the pigeon and took it away and set it down at the curb.

She touched her glasses again and watched the

buses passing. "There are many buses here," she said. "The fumes are bad."

"Do they bother you?"

"It is my job, so I do not let them bother me."

He nodded his head. "Tell me, what do you do in Krakow? What is your occupation?"

"I do not live in Krakow. I live in Warsaw."

"And what do you do in Warsaw?"

"I am an instructor in literature at the University of Warsaw."

"You are here for the summer?"

"I have been visiting in America all summer. I work at temporary jobs. But I return to Poland in three days, tomorrow after tomorrow."

"The day after tomorrow." As soon as he corrected her he was sorry. Had he grown so precise that even this woman had to be summarily corrected? He closed his eyes.

"Tomorrow after tomorrow is not correct? My English is not good."

"Yes, it is correct. Your English is very good."

"I shall leave for Poland on that date, on Capitol Airlines, first to New York, that is Wednesday, no? Today is Monday, is it not?

"Yes," he said, looking at his watch.

She was about to turn away when suddenly she spoke to him again.

"And you? Do you live here in Chicago? And your occupation?"

"Yes, I do. I'm a law professor at one of the universities."

She smiled at him. "You are also an academician?"

"Yes, I am also an academician."

A young boy came to the tables passing out hand-bills advertising a prizefight that night at the stadium. He took one and she peered over his shoulder at the handbill.

"Would you like to go to the fights tonight?" he said. He couldn't believe that he had suddenly said that to her.

"Fights? Boxing?" She was reading the handbill over his shoulder. "No, it's very expensive."

"No, I'm inviting you. I will pay for you. You will be my guest."

She pushed at her glasses and squinted. "No. It is a brutal sport and I do not like it, but thank you. Thank you very much indeed." She smiled down at him and turned and walked back to the warming table and put her coffee pot down.

He couldn't believe that he'd asked her. It was such a foolish request. He had no interest in prizefighting. It was a clumsy invitation and she'd rejected him.

He left her a dollar tip fluttering under a spoon. She approached him and stood by the table as he rose to leave. "That is too much money. It is too much as a tip for only coffee."

"Keep it and spend it in Warsaw," he said, extending his hand.

She shook it with a quick, formal gesture.

"Thank you. Thank you very much indeed."

"Good luck, Maria," he told her as he walked away. He had the notion that she was watching him as he walked down State Street, but he didn't look back. He knew the name of one other noble Polish family, the Kossak family. In his apartment, he had a painting by Juliusz Kossak of a tall man in a black silk hat, on a white horse. He didn't mention the Kossak painting to her; he didn't even mention the platypuses.

That evening, after dinner, he returned to his office to work on the book. His desk was piled with papers and books. The cleaning lady, a heavy, round-faced woman named Stanislawa, was slapping at his papers with a dust cloth.

"Stanislawa, don't touch any of that stuff."

"Professor Strauss, you always say same thing: 'Stanislawa, no touch this, no touch that.' Who cleans if I don't touch?"

It was their regular evening routine. He pretended to be angry with her and then he would sit and watch her dust. He turned the stereo on to a classical station and sat back in his chair.

"Stanislawa, are you Polish?"

"Yes, I am Polish."

"I have met a Polish woman."

"Good for you." She had her back to him and kept on working.

"No, seriously. Very beautiful, very intelligent, a waitress in a restaurant downtown. She's an instructor at the University of Warsaw visiting here for the summer." He turned the stereo down. The announcer was saying something about the Amsterdam Concertgebouw. "But she's leaving for Poland the day after tomorrow."

Stanislawa looked up at him. "She not waitress."

"What do you mean?"

"She not waitress. She spider."

"I don't understand."

"Beautiful Polish girl come to Chicago. Leave university in Warsaw. Work as waitress in America. She come here to spider."

"Spy?"

"Yah, sure. Spider for Poland."

He sat up in the chair and lit a cigarette.

"You shouldn't smoke so much, Professor Strauss. Such bad habit. My son he quit three years ago. He just say, 'Mama, I quit,' and he quit."

He waved the smoke away from her.

"You think she's a spy?"

"Yah, of course. Last year two beautiful young girls from Poland come work here for summer on cleaning crew. You were away. Say to me all the time, every night, 'Stanislawa, why you like America? You come back to Poland with us. You live like queen there on social security. America no good.' I tell them, 'You crazy? You not cleaning girls, you come to America to spider for Poland. You beautiful young smart girls. Spiders. Leave Stanislawa alone.' "

She moved out of his office, using the feather duster on his walls. At the doorway she turned to him. "You stay away from Polish girl, Professor Strauss. She leave in two days anyway. She be trapped in Poland. Soon all Poland like prison." She snapped her fingers. "I know." She closed his door and he heard her vacuuming in the corridor.

He tried to work but his mind was not on work, so he headed down to a tavern where he could meet some people and talk. It was almost eight o'clock. On the way out he stopped in the lobby to stare at the brass cylinder replica of the Code of Hammurabi. There really were platypuses and scarabs inscribed on the scroll and also human figures. He touched the scroll with his finger, this ancient secret Braille. He closed his eyes and tried to discern some intelligence through his fingertips. He didn't feel anything except a Braille of metal. Someone had used the same kind of human figures on one of our space shots, a metal plate on the side of the rocket with an American flag and the figures of a man and a woman. After two thousand years we were still doing the same thing—inscribing stick figures of men and women on metal plates—except now we were shooting them out into space.

There were several law students in the tavern and one of them, a young woman in a blouse and jeans skirt, with clouds of frizzed blonde hair, sat down with him. He remembered her first name, Allison, and that she was in his Conflicts class last year, and once he'd bought her a drink.

"The ice cream truck in my neighborhood keeps playing the same song over and over again."

"What's the name of the song?" he asked her.

"I think it's Cielito Lindo."

"Can you whistle a few lines?"

She whistled a little; he nodded.

"What did you do this summer, Allison?"

"Well, I spent five weeks at Oxford." She smiled and pushed herself back from the table. "Studying German expressionism with this marvelous old professor, who was almost stone deaf. I'd bicycle to his house and a maid would usher me in and bring us tea and scones. Then I'd spend the hour shouting into his one good ear, 'Professor Tillofson, do you, sir, remember the Edvard Muench exhibit in Paris in 1892?' Of course, Tillofson wasn't that old. But he always claimed he remembered everything. 'The Muench exhibition? Oh, rah-ther,' " she said, mimicking his accent and blinking. "Have you ever had scones, Paul? I also sang madrigals in the chapel. I love English madrigals."

"Can you sing me a madrigal?"

She sang a piece of a madrigal in a high pleasant voice and looked at him. "Paul, you're in a bitchy mood."

"I'm sorry."

"I read your article in the Michigan Law Review," she said.

"What did you think of it?"

"Can you whistle me a bar of it?"

He laughed and whistled for her. "Does it sound anything like Cielito Lindo?"

"It was mostly all pure academic bullshit, you know. Very little of it made sense to me or any of my friends, Paul."

*   *   *

A half hour later he was on the subway on his way downtown. A nun of about 35 sat down beside him. Neither of them spoke, and the train jostled them as they sped through the dark tunnel under the Chicago River. He stared straight ahead at the graffiti on the back of the seat in front of him: "Las Aguilas," "Mondo," "L/K's." When they came out of the tunnel and stopped at Randolph Street she moved her legs aside into the aisle and he brushed past her as he left the train. "God bless you," she said to him quietly.

He came up the escalator onto State Street; it was quite cold. He saw Maria standing against a wall across the street reading a newspaper, and walked over to her.

"I've come for another cup of coffee."

She put the paper down and smiled at him. The

wind was blowing through her hair. "Please sit down. I've had almost no customers because of the cool weather."

"Why do you stay out here, then? Why don't you go inside?"

"The owners forbid it. They say I must remain outside at my station. I am fortunate to have this sweater, my friend's sweater." She was wearing a brown sweater and as she talked she kept her arms folded around herself, but she was shivering.

He sat down under an umbrella and put his raincoat on, and he was warm enough. She'd been outside for several hours. When she returned with the coffee he apologized to her for asking her to the fights.

"Oh, that is perfectly all right. It was kind of you to ask me."

He watched some buses passing along State Street behind her.

"Would you care to have a glass of wine with me this evening, Maria?"

"This evening?" She hesitated. "Yes, I would like that very much indeed, but I must remain here until 9:30."

"Well, good. I'll come back for you."

"At 9:30 I will be available to meet you. I was going to go shopping and then meet my friends from Poland. If I may please be back at 11:30, I will go with you."

"If you have shopping. . . . "

"No, no, the shopping is not important. I will be very pleased to meet with you. Together we shall have a glass of wine."

When he returned he didn't see her standing outside. The tables were empty. He went inside and the dining room was crowded and alive with conversation.

She was standing with a man and a woman at the cashier's counter. He hardly recognized her. She was dressed in a navy blue blazer with a blue silk ascot and a black shoulder bag. She was wearing a blue dress and white stockings.

"This is my friend Paul," she said to them. "I would like you to meet Mr. and Mrs. Patel. They're from Pakistan and they are the owners of this restaurant." He shook hands with each of them. "I shall return at 11:30. That is my situation," she said to them and walked out ahead of him.

"I was looking for you in uniform."

"Oh, I hate that uniform." She was tall and slender and walked gracefully with long strides just a step ahead of him. "And I don't like those people."

"You look lovely."

"Thank you. I bought these clothes in London last year."

"You were in London?"

"Yes." She remained quiet and walked with her arms folded. After they crossed Lake Street under the El tracks, she turned to him. "Do you have a house?" she suddenly asked him.

"A house? No, I live in an apartment."

"With whom do you live in your apartment?"

"I live by myself."

Her skin was so fair he could see her blushing. She nodded and kept on walking, but she looked at him once and her eyes seemed to flash.

They crossed the Michigan Avenue bridge. There were crowds of people and the buildings were ablaze with light reflected on the dark water of the river. Traffic rumbled all around them as they crossed the bridge. They sat in the arcade of the Wrigley Building by a fountain and beds of petunias. She sat beside him on a slatted bench overlooking the flower beds.

"Your brown sweater," he said to her.

"Yes?"

"It's a man's sweater."

"A man's sweater?" She looked at him with a half smile.

"It's not your sweater?"

"No, it is a friend's sweater," she said.

"And you also have an apartment?"

"Yes, but the apartment is not where I have borrowed the sweater. I procure the sweater elsewhere and only for cold nights."

"Oh," he said, and she smiled again at him slightly.

"The sweater does not reside in your apartment?"

She looked directly at him.

"No, it does not reside in my apartment."

He took a deep breath, inhaling the scent of the flowers, as they both watched an excursion boat passing under the bridge.

They went for a drink to the top of the Hancock Building, a hundred floors up, where they could look down on the city. From their table at the window they could see lines of traffic streaming along the Outer Drive; the road was edged by the blackness of Lake Michigan. Planes were moving along the horizon in landing patterns as they headed toward O'Hare Airport. A trio was playing softly at a small dance floor behind the bar. They each ordered a glass of white wine.

"Chicago, it is a beautiful city," she said, staring out at the lights beneath them. "A very powerful city."

"Is it like any city in Poland?"

"Like a city in Poland? No, Poland's cities are un-like Chicago."

"Do you have family there?"

"I have a mother and a younger sister. My father died when I was a child. He died of leukoymia, is that correct?"

"Leukemia, yes. What is your last name, Maria?"

"My family name is Czestoszewicz. It is difficult for Americans." She took a pen from her purse and wrote her name in neat letters on a cocktail napkin. C.z.e.s.t.o.s.z.e.w.i.c.z.

"My name is Strauss. Paul Strauss." He wrote his name beside hers on the napkin. S.t.r.a.u.s.s.

"That is a German name?"

"Yes, but I am Jewish."

"Oh," she said, "Paul Strauss," pronouncing each name emphatically.

"Do you know any Jews in Poland?"

"Very few. Most of the Jews left in 1968 under Gomulka."

"We are an unusual combination."

She glanced at him again. "Yes, apparently." She opened her purse and began looking through it and handed him a photograph of a woman, an older woman seated on a couch with two portraits behind her. "That is my mother. Her name is Theresa, and behind her are portraits of my great-grandparents. No, my grandparents. I always confuse those designations." She gave him another photo. "And this is my dog Alex." She tapped the photograph of the dog. "He is a male dog." She handed him another. "This is Alex and me at a dog forum in Krakow."

"A dog show."

"Yes, a dog show. And this is my sister Katarzyna. She is fifteen and very intelligent."

She watched him as he examined the photograph. The sister looked like Maria.

She took a folder of scenes of Krakow from her purse and handed it to him. "You will take this, please. A gift."

"Thank you."

"I will be there in two days. I do not need this folder anymore."

"Thank you very much. Would you write something on the inside?"

She looked out at the planes heading away over the lake. She wrote, "For Paul from Maria, 21.09.81, Chicago." She paused, and as she gave him the folder she said to herself, "Tak."

" 'Tak' is a Polish word?"

"Tak is yes."

"Tak," he said to her.

They each drank their wine and listened to the music. Some people began moving toward the dance floor.

"Would you care to dance, Maria?" he asked her.

"Dahnce?" She repeated the word in her English accent. "I am prepared to dance."

He stood up and gestured toward the dance floor and held her chair. She walked ahead of him very formally to the floor and turned to him and held out her arms. He held her lightly, barely moving to the music. He put his face against her face and he coud feel the flutter of her eyelashes and soft scent of her perfume and he lost himself in the fragrance. Neither of them spoke. He hadn't been this alive with feeling in months. This beautiful Polish woman had suddenly made him want to feel again. When the number ended, his lips brushed a strand of her hair along her cheek.

"Thank you, Paul, for a lovely dahnce," she said to him with a slight bow.

"You're welcome."

"I have danced infrequently since I left Warsaw and the university."

"You have dances at the university?"

"Not the university, but we frequent discos elsewhere."

"I will show you my university from the window. Come," he said to her. She stood beside him and he pointed down at a cluster of lights. "That's the law school where I teach."

She leaned her head toward the window. She held her scarf at her throat as she peered over the railing.

"Would you like to go there? I believe we have time," he said.

"Go to see your university?" She was staring down at the lights.

"Yes, it's not quite ten-thirty. I'll show you my office, my place of work."

"Very well, Paul, " she said, looking up at him. "I will go. I will be pleased to go."

They took a cab to the law school. There were two women students coming down the stairs of the library, one in jeans and the other in white coveralls. They both were carrying book bags and cans of soft drink. The student in coveralls was talking about her friend who had sent a postcard from Sri Lanka where she was working

with Sri Lankan women for a year forming conscious-
ness-raising groups. The two women recognized him
and smiled. Maria walked ahead of him into the corridor and began looking at some of the oil portraits and
display cases. She stood with her arms folded at each
portrait and examined the face. There was a gallery of
photographs of judges and prominent teachers and
members of government. He sat on a bench and lit a
cigarette.

"This room is modeled after an English inn of
court. The entire building is," he said to her.

"Yes, it is quite antique."

"Is it like a building at Warsaw University?"

"No, it is more like Krakow. Warsaw is in the modern style."

He watched her from the bench. "What do you
think of our judges and officials?"

"They're all very nice."

"Yes. . . . "

"No, very nice. Very conservative looking."

"But what?"

She turned with her arms folded and cocked her
head. "There are no women. It is difficult to see."

"No, I believe there are women."

"You do not permit women lawyers?"

"We have many women lawyers."

She smiled again and held her fingers together.
"But they are not permitted status as judges and
officials."

"No, they have status as judges and officials."

"Ah," she said and turned away from the gallery
of photographs.

They walked up another flight of stairs to his office.

Stanislawa was wiping the staircase railings and didn't see them coming until they were on her landing.

"Stanislawa, I want you to meet someone."

The scrub woman was bent over and her face was red from exertion. She folded her rag and slowly stood up and looked at Maria.

"This is the woman I told you about."

"How do you do?" Stanislawa said formally in English in a low voice and looked at the floor.

He put his arm around Stanislawa and whispered. "Ask her if she's a spider."

Maria shook Stanislawa's hand.

"Stanislawa much work to do, Professor Strauss." She began wiping at the railing again. "Bye bye, it was nice meeting with you," she said as she moved down the stairs away from them.

He invited Maria into his office and began making coffee. He pushed the papers off his couch and she sat down with her purse over her knees and watched him.

"This is a nice room."

"This is my office."

"It is yours alone? I have never had my own office. Even our professors must share."

"No, it is mine alone. These are all mine." He gestured at the mound of papers on his desk.

"And what is your field, Paul?"

"International law. Conflicts of law."

She nodded and held herself over her knees.

"I am trying to write a book," he said to her.

She looked pleased. "I am also writing a manuscript, what you call a thesis. I have the manuscript in Poland. I carry it with me in my head. Do you know Czeslaw Milosz? He is a poet and an essayist in Berkeley, California. He won the Nobel Prize in 1980. He is from Poland. I am writing on him."

"I have heard of Milosz but I do not know his work."

"He has a very dark vision of America."

"And you, Maria, do you share this vision?"

"Tak," she said, clasping her knees. "Perhaps we should not talk politics. I am a guest in your country. Do you know Solzhenitsyn? He is in America too and he shares this dark vision of Milosz." She smiled and rocked. "You have phonograph records here. Tell me, suddenly you seem very sad, Paul."

"I am not sad."

"Is it some woman who makes you sad?" She was teasing him. It was perhaps the first time.

"A woman? No, I am too neurotic to be sad over a woman."

"Erotic?"

"No, neurotic. It is the opposite."

"You are not erotic?"

He smiled at her. "I am not erotic."

"You have been married, Paul?"

"Yes, some years ago, but I am divorced."

"Your wife is not in America?"

"No, she is in America, but I am out of touch with her. Perhaps I'm not in America."

"Oh," she said, ignoring his remark. Often if she didn't understand the nuances of a remark she would just ignore it. She stood and pointed to a photograph. "You are on the cricket team."

"Baseball. I'm on the faculty baseball team. It's a main event here."

"You have a refrigerator." She pointed again.

"Yes, do you want some soup? I can make us some soup. What is your favorite soup?"

"Cucumber soup. Do you have any?"

"No, we're out of cucumber soup. What is the Polish word for coffee?"

"Kava."

"The kava is ready." He poured her a cup of coffee. "Tell me, Maria, are you interested in marriage? Is it something that's part of your life plan? In America everyone has a life plan."

"Life plan?"

"Everyone has an inner chart of their lives."

"Of course, I am inner charted." She sat up and crossed her legs. "I am not determined always to be a doctor of literature. Instead, I would like to be a wife and have a family. I love children."

"You know, if you married an American citizen you would not have to leave the country. You could apply for permanent residency."

"Do you know an American citizen who will marry me?"

"I know one such person," he said to her, putting down his coffee, "but he is much too erotic for marriage."

*   *   *

They went down the hall into a deserted classroom. He didn't turn on the lights because the room was illuminated by moonlight. It looked in the half light like the sanctuary of a church and the rows of seats resembled rows of pews. He walked her down the row that led to the lectern.

"Stand here, please." He switched on the microphone. "I will sit up there."

He walked back up the rows of empty seats and sat in the last row. The room was cavernous, with benches of dark wood and portraits of 17th and 18th century English jurists. He sat just below the portraits almost hidden in the shadows.

"Now tell me of your dark vision of America," he called down to her.

"No. I am not here to lecture on America."

"Will you say something for the folks into the microphone?"

"What shall I say?" She scratched the microphone with her fingernail.

"Whatever comes to your mind."

"I have already said what I have to say."

"What is the Polish word for friend?"

"Friend? Przyjaciel."

"Can't you say friend?"

She leaned over. "Przyjaciel."

"Try something else."

"Dobry wieczor." Her voice echoed up to him.

"What's that?"

"Good evening."

She snapped off the microphone and walked up the row toward him. She extended her hand to him. "Paul?" she called up to him in the darkness.

"Yes."

"I can't see you, Paul."

"I'm over here."

"Is this where you teach your class?"

"Yes, I teach a class here."

"Then we are violating the dignity of your classroom, are we not?"

*   *   *

In the cab on the way downtown, he took her hand but she wouldn't look at him. She sat stiffly at the window, staring at the people along the walks. Just before they arrived at the restaurant he asked if he could see her again tomorrow.

"It will be quite difficult," she said. She turned away from the window and looked at him. "But I will arrange it. I can spend perhaps two hours in the afternoon. It is my last day in America. I am not even prepared."

He felt like putting his arms around her, but she was very formal and reserved. When they reached the cafe two of her friends were standing outside, a short young man in white shirt and black bow tie, and another woman. He asked the cab to wait and she introduced them. "This is Tadeusz, who is from my hometown of Krakow and will take my job here." They shook hands. "And this is Krystyna, who is my good friend." Krystyna, an attractive slender woman with sunglasses on top of her head, shook his hand.

Maria walked with him back to the cab. "We shall meet again tomorrow then, Paul."

"Why don't you come to my class at two o'clock?"

"Very good. I will come to your class."

"You can catch the bus. Number sixty-three will drop you right in front of the law school." He took a pen and wrote down the address on his card.

She looked at the card. "See you then," she said.

*   *   *

That night, for the first time in weeks, he cleaned

his apartment. He actually did some dishes and threw out food that had rotted in the refrigerator. He mixed a shot of scotch and a glass of milk before he went to sleep, and slept well, not waking up every two hours as he had the last few nights. In the morning, refreshed, he put on a dark suit and noticed that one of the seams was beginning to split above the right pocket. He took a black ball point and colored the fissure of the split seam. He was being fastidious again. When he searched for a pair of black socks, he found two scummy plates under his bed, gray fuzz growing on them like clumps of penicillin. He also found some research notes. He threw the plates down the incinerator and put the notes in his briefcase. Instead of his usual cup of freeze-dried coffee, he had a leisurely breakfast in a drug store on Michigan Avenue. After breakfast he bought a package of hand-cut reeds for his clarinet.

At the afternoon lecture he saw her come in, almost at the close, and shyly take a seat at the rear of the room. It was almost the same seat he'd sat in the night before. He was gesticulating when he saw her and he felt himself flush, his face growing wet with perspiration. She was dressed in the blue jacket she'd worn the evening before, but now she was wearing a different scarf. He thought of introducing her to the class, but he didn't. He was talking about the decline of the Hobbsian view of the competitive battle of "all against all." Now he heard himself talking about Samuel Johnson—how isolated and compartmentalized all of us really are— the day of Economic Legal Man and self-aggrandizement was drawing to a close—we were in the last decades of the century . . . moving into the era of Philosophic Legal Man and Woman. A new Humanism was surely coming forward now and would determine these last two decades of the law and perhaps the future of the world. What was for the greater good of the world community would of necessity prevail if civilization was to survive. He thought of mentioning the Solidarity Union in Poland. He looked up at her. He stopped gesturing. He could, perhaps, introduce her to the class: "This is Maria Czestoszewicz, who is returning to Poland tomorrow." No, it would be very embarrassing for her.

One of the women in the first row was watching him now, and she turned around and stared up at Maria. The woman was a student he'd had coffee with last week, Elizabeth, yes Elizabeth, and he'd thought then of quietly asking her to go for a drink, but he hadn't. Elizabeth had told him she'd spent the summer at a cello school in Scotland in an old manor house in the countryside outside Edinburgh. One night while practicing she'd looked out the window and seen a silver puma in the moonlight. "Crawling along the cliffs. . . . " His hand was now trembling slightly and he shoved it in his pocket. There was no sense in seeking accommodation with a woman who ran with silver pumas in the moonlight. Soon she'd be like a puma at his throat. "God bless you," the nun had said to him.

After class he didn't take his customary questions, and he immediately left with Maria. He wanted to take her to Marshall Field's. There were crowds of shoppers on the first floor when they arrived at Field's and they rode the escalator to the third floor. A young saleswoman in the sportswear department approached them.

"I would like you to show my friend a sweater," he told her.

"Paul, I will not accept."

"You will accept. It will be my pleasure."

"No, I refuse." She fingered the price tag of a sweater on a manikin. "It is much too expensive, fifty dollars. It is out of the question."

The young saleswoman stood by patiently and then excused herself.

"Maria, this is a gift. Please, just look at them. I'll hold your jacket and your purse."

She seemed annoyed with him. She also seemed very sad. She explained that she had what the Germans call travel fever. She used a German word, the fever that travelers have just before they leave.

He watched her move cautiously along the racks of clothing. There were many women customers, pleasant-looking, well-dressed American women. She seemed like a strange interloper, almost like a nervous young animal.

She came back to him and handed him her jacket and purse and reluctantly tried on one sweater. Her face was very red. The sweater was a full-sleeved crew neck. She looked like a slender schoolboy.

"I will not buy it," she said to him, posing in front of him. She had one foot forward in a model's stance and she turned slowly.

"It looks nice on you." It was shown with a blouse. "You could also buy the blouse."

She flashed an annoyed look at him and went down to a full-length mirror and stood among the women and inspected herself in the sweater. She stood for a long time and then with a shrug walked over and selected a different sweater, a heavier cardigan, and took it off the hanger. She came back, and without saying anything pulled the original sweater over her head. Her glasses fell to the floor. She handed the sweater to him and put her glasses back on, and then tried the cardigan on. When her glasses fell she reminded him of a high-cheekboned beautiful Dutch girl he remembered in a painting by Vermeer. She went back to the mirror and posed again. She posed in all the sections of the mirror. The young saleswoman noticed her and stood by, watching. Finally Maria returned to him.

"I will pay for hahlf," she said very seriously.

"No, you will not pay for half. I will pay for the sweater."

*   *   *

In the restaurant they sat over coffee and croissants. Most of the customers were young women executives who had come across the street from the bank for late afternoon coffee. They were dressed in expensive suits with silk ties and blouses. The room was filled with their laughter and the sound of their voices.

"The coffee is very good," she said to him. The sweater was in a box at her feet.

"You know, Maria, you don't have to leave America. You can apply for an extension of your visitor's visa. Perhaps you can even apply for a student visa. You could change to student status and go to Berkeley and study with Milosz."

"Perhaps someday," she said quietly. "You must in any case apply for the student visa from your own country. I would have to apply from Poland."

"You could just ask for an extension of your visitor's visa. At least you'd be able to stay here while the application was pending."

She didn't answer him, and watched the women at the adjoining tables.

"Why not continue to work here for a few months, particularly until the situation in Poland stabilizes?"

She picked at her roll. "No, my mother is expecting me. Anyway, here I am a second-class citizen. If I remain I will not be given a chance at citizenship. I will always be an illegal. The Americans exploit the illegals and use them for cheap labor. It is not a life. I will never be free. I would rather be in Poland."

"Do you think that Solidarity will prevail in Poland?"

"I think there will be an accommodation with the government and Solidarnosc will prevail. Yes. I think that."

"Russia will permit this?"

"They have no choice." She looked up at him. "They have one war already in Afghanistan. They do not want a civil war in Poland."

She sipped her coffee and stared at the women across from her.

He touched her signet ring with his index finger. "Your family name, does it have a meaning?"

"It means in English 'from Czestochowa.' It is a city near Krakow."

"I don't know Czestochowa."

"It is the city of the shrine of the Black Madonna. Have you heard, Paul, of the Black Madonna of Czestochowa? It is an icon that is used—how do you say—to repel the invaders of Poland."

He could see her eyes were glistening. Now would be the time to ask her to marry him. He could ask her very simply. "Maria, I would like you to marry me. If you marry me, you will be given priority for American citizenship." It was an easy solution—a simple reaching out—and he could save her. If she returned to Poland, she would be trapped there forever like an insect in a plastic cube. He watched her picking at the croissant. His hand was trembling again. Why couldn't he help her? Why was he so self-involved that he couldn't do this for her? Solidarity wasn't going to prevail. The Poles were so romantic. She'd be squashed like a bug under Russian tank treads. He heard a voice speaking so deep inside his head that it was unintelligible, but the words wouldn't come. He didn't say anything to her. He was too cool and laconic to throw a romantic gesture like that at her. Maybe this winter he'd fly there and visit her. Take a skiing vacation. Or perhaps next summer.

"Do they have skiing in Poland in winter? Is there a good place?"

"Yes, at Zakopane. It is on the border near Czechoslovakia."

"Perhaps this winter I will come to Zakopane for skiing and we will meet there."

"You will come to visit in Poland?" She touched at her eye with a napkin.

"I would like to see you again."

"Yes, I would like that."

"Or perhaps you will get another visa next year, Maria."

"Oh, yes, I would like very much to come to America again. I will apply to Berkeley at California to study with Milosz." She brightened. "We could meet in California, Paul. There are beaches there, I understand. Do you like the seaside?"

She touched her hair and pushed at her glasses. "Are there beaches in Poland?"

"Yes, of course. There is a lovely beach at Sopot, near Gdansk. There is amber there. Pieces of amber wash up on the shore and you can pick them out of the sand. I remember also the pine forest. When I was a child my father often took me to Sopot. In the forest they had a dancing bear in a cage. Some day perhaps I will have a little house there by the seaside."

"We could meet next summer in Sopot, Maria."

"Perhaps," she said, "we will meet at Sopot."

*   *   *

At the outdoor cafe her friend Tadeusz was standing at the tables in his white shirt and black bow tie. He bowed when he saw them approaching. She had written her name and address on a card, and he had given her another card with his phone number on it. "Thank you, Paul," she said when he handed her the card.

"I have always had a dream, Maria, that someday I would go with some of my friends to eastern Europe and play jazz. I play the clarinet in a jazz band. We would come, of course, to Warsaw. Is there a hotel in Warsaw where we could play American jazz?"

"The Hotel Viktoria. It would be such a place."

"How do you write 'Dear Maria'?" he asked.

"Droga Maria."

"Would you write it down for me?"

She wrote Droga Maria beside her address. The wind blew her hair. He took her in his arms and kissed her on the cheek and then moved his lips to her mouth. She returned his kiss for just one second and turned her face.

"I will come to Warsaw," he said. "Perhaps we will play at the Viktoria some day soon."

She shook his hand. "If you come to Warsaw with your jazz band, Paul, I will be your impresario." She smiled at him. "I will write to you, Paul. Please write to me." She turned quickly and walked into the restaurant and she was gone.

He was alone again, with his platypuses and the silver puma.

THE CHRISTMAS PARTY

Albert Winston. There he is. Standing by the punch bowl. Peaches and champagne. Albert Winston. Tall. Myopic. Horn rims and black vest. Harvard Law, 1957. Winston is responsible for color coordinating the office reception room in beige and brown. He also began the policy of having the receptionist offer the clients coffee or a soft drink as they entered. "May I bring you coffee, or perhaps a Tab? A Coke? Nothing? How about one of these magazines?" she'll say with a concerned smile, looking up from her IBM. A pretty frosted blonde, a short sculptured haircut and plastic earphones trailing. "No magazines then?" Albert Winston buys *Town and Country* and *Gentleman's Quarterly* for the reception desk. It is rumored that he's homosexual. There's no evidence other than a preference for folios of Da Vinci drawings that he occasionally leaves on the floor after his nap. He's posing now for Schloma Herzl, a tall Israeli girl who's in the States on a visitor's visa as an international law specialist. Schloma points to her camera and Albert Winston holds his glass up and smiles. He bends her back in an exaggerated embrace, so suddenly that the sunglasses on her hair fall to the floor. He releases her and grins. Albert Winston is no homosexual, it says to the kids from the mailroom standing next to the peaches and champagne. Now he's wearing her dark glasses and Schloma takes another picture.

Schloma Herzl. Who came to Chicago the week of the Yom Kippur war. Who has an apartment in Marina City with a Lebanese chartered accountant. They keep a tank of piranhas in the living room next to Schloma's Chanukah bush. On the door in tiny gold letters is printed "Hakmir Lhafistan, C.P.A. and Miss Schloma Herzl." Schloma is rumored to be having an affair with Mr. Lee Trevelyan of Antitrust. International Department secretaries never accompany Antitrust people to Washington, but last week Trevelyan signed Schloma out for three days at the Mayflower in Washington and two days at the Barclay in Manhattan. Schloma came back flushed and with her hair in high coils like an Assyrian dancing girl. Trevelyan immediately left for the holidays with his family for their townhouse in Scottsdale.

Watson Haywood III. Trial lawyer extraordinaire. Now he's posing for Schloma. "Watts" Haywood is about fifty-eight and looks like FDR if FDR could have by some grace arisen from his wheelchair and stood grinning at the fringe of an office Christmas party. Diffident, patrician, he nods and bites on his cigarette holder, a lank of salt and pepper hair over the fine forehead. But when Haywood smiles, his teeth are so heavily stained with tobacco he looks as if he chews betel nut. Later he does a long slow dance with Schloma and kisses her ear and offers to drive her home. When she insists on waiting for Lhafistan, Haywood goes back into his office and opens a bottle of J&B and sits brooding with the lights off, drinking and throwing darts at his board by the moonlight that filters through the Levolor blinds.

Enid Carlsson. She of the switchboard and the soft drinks. The perfect nose. The perfect chin. Framed to fit the square of the receptionist glass by Albert Winston, interior decorator. He thinks she completes the picture and looks like a Breck girl. Actually, she's very tough and at night reads feminist fiction, currently *Bitches and Sad Ladies*, while her boyfriend, Peter Rebeschini, goes to law school. During the day she offers coffee and Coke, and Peter is a clerk for the firm. When Rebeschini goes to court, he calls the office from a booth in the Federal Building and reads poetry to Enid. Today, John Donne: " . . . no man is an island entire unto himself . . . " Enid blushes behind the plastic earphones and stacks of *Gentleman's Quarterly*. She also writes poems on yellow legal pads and hands him folded notes. Her first lines are usually song titles, "You Light Up My Life . . . you do."

Arthur Bates-Vonier. Senior Partner. Eminent international labor lawyer. His jowls tremble with laughter reflected in the light of the blazing cognac over the Baked Alaska. An Oriental chef from Don Ho's in a white chef's hat and apron shakes more cognac at the blue flames. The lights are off and everyone is singing. Bates-Vonier stands with his hands over his stomach. In the blue-etched shadows he looks like an ancient Kabuki performer, chalk-faced and beady-eyed. Standing before his staff, he is singing "I wish you a Merry Christmas . . . " Last week he flew to London and lunched at Gray's Inn where he delivered a paper on the revision of the NATO arbitration convention and stole a silver cup rumored to have belonged to Lord Birkenhead. He smuggled the cup back to Chicago in his briefcase and has it hidden in a velvet bag on his bookshelf.

Gray's Inn has issued a bulletin. Bates-Vonier has failed to respond. He may yet mail the cup back. He hasn't made up his mind. The cognac glow is dying. Bates-Vonier sings louder.

Horace Kelly. Another Senior Partner. His wife resembles a pit bulldog. They winter in Palm Springs. This year they're headed for a cruise to the Galapagos to witness a perfect eclipse of the sun. After the Galapagos cruise, the Kellys will return to Palm Springs where they'll spend the winter months gardening and walking. He plays gin rummy. She plays canasta. On Thursdays, he secretly goes to an exclusive massage parlor in the desert owned by a Chicago politician where he has a personal masseuse, Coleen, a young green-eyed Irish girl from Tucson. Each Thursday, talcumed and dressed in a polo shirt and shorts, a happy Horace Kelly slips Coleen a crisp one-hundred-dollar bill and pats her cheek as he heads out toward his gray Mercedes. Mrs. Kelly is now standing between Horace and Bates-Vonier like a wary referee as they watch the chef flame the Baked Alaska. Horace Kelly is angry with Bates-Vonier because Vonier has been usurping the firm's limousine. There is one firm limousine, a 1975 black eight-passenger Cadillac with jumpseats, private telephone, and bar. It's usually available to Horace Kelly, but Bates-Vonier has requisitioned the limo twice this month, the last time on his return from London with Lord Birkenhead's cup. That was the night Horace and his wife were headed for the opening of the Stuttgart Ballet. They were to pick up the president of Citibank and his wife. Horace Kelly rang for the car and the garage informed him it had been dispatched to O'Hare to pick up Vonier. Horace and the president of Citibank

and their wives had to cab it to the Stuttgart with a cab-
bie who burned incense in his ashtray. Horace isn't
speaking to Bates-Vonier, but won't tell him why.

Kenneth Stopsworth. Senior Associate. Dunks two
cups in the champagne (there are no more peaches).
One he drinks immediately. The second he holds and
sips. Good old Ken Stopsworth. When a partner dies it's
Stopsworth who cleans out his office. Shreds the package of old love letters before the widow arrives. Dumps
the pornographic pictures. Plucks exotic names and
numbers from the man's private Rolodex. Good old Ken
Stopsworth. "Fa la la la la . . . "

Marjorie Hackberry. Paralegal. Long hair, shoulder purses, suede jackets, always heavily scented. She
has just come from her office after having written 150
interrogatories in a suit involving the shipment of caviar
from Interlux (a division of the Byelorussian government) to a Chicago hotel. Her first questions to Interlux. "State your name." "State your age." "Where do
you reside?" "Are you married?" "How many children
born of the marriage?" She's turned the wrong switch
on the magcard typewriter. Question No. 96: "State the
weight in kilograms of one jar of Interlux Caviar (A) ordinary lumpfish (B) deluxe lumpfish." Question No. 97:
"If you are accusing your wife of adultery, name a
specific time, place, and cohabiter." The Byelorussian
government will be amused.

William Toomlin. Blond Guards' mustache. Ex-
Green Beret. He's already spent his $6,000 Christmas
bonus. Four years with the firm, $40,000 salary, but he's
overdrawn $18,000. The executive committee has asked
Toomlin to pay back the $18,000 "as soon as reasonably
convenient or, if not in a lump sum, in installments with

interest over a fixed period of time." A note to Toomlin on office stationery was delivered this morning by a messenger in a separate envelope along with his Christmas bonus. Toomlin, who owes American Express $3,500 for last year's trip to New Zealand, immediately mailed his bonus check to Billy Taber, a Chicago real-estate developer with a tennis club in Costa Rica. Toomlin is buying a tennis condo in the mountains outside San Jose. On Christmas Day, he's booked a flight to San Jose where he's meeting Carla Juarez de Costa-Rivera. Juarez de Costa-Rivera is a law professor—black eyes, olive skin, black hair, leather gaucho pants—from Guayaquil who's counsel with Toomlin on a brief for Amnesty International accusing the government of Peru of torture. She has arranged through contacts for Toomlin to interview the attorney general of Peru in Lima. Toomlin will dictate a briefing memo on the plane (copy CIA, copy Justice, copy State-Latin Affairs). If he can spring some prisoners, Toomlin has been told the CIA will cover the $6,000 he's blown on the tennis condo. He's angry that his condominium deposit should somehow have gotten intertwined with his overdrawn account and the question of torture of political prisoners in Peru, but still he's feeling good about the trip. He has his eyes closed to the singing because he's trying to meditate.

Marcia Houbignant. Black. Hoop earrings. Twenty-six. Divorced. Former Assistant U.S. Attorney. She and William Toomlin are now dancing in a far corner of the room. He holds her stiffly, his arm just touching the small of her back. She laughs shyly. They move in and out of the long shadows of the room. Suddenly they're gone.

Corliss Bagby. Estate Planner. He's dispatched 150 "Harry and David" poinsettia plants to the firm's most important estate clients, the widows in Palm Beach, Palm Springs, Tucson. William Toomlin's secretary prevailed upon Cor Bagby's secretary to divert a poinsettia and send it to Carla Juarez in Guayaquil. It arrived yesterday. The card read "With warm personal regards for a joyous holiday season, Corliss Bagby III." Juarez De Costa-Rivera hasn't the slightest idea who Corliss Bagby is and has given the plant to her maid, a placid Inca woman who, unknown to Juarez, is a courier for the Peruvian Military Triumvirate. She has given it to them. Cor Bagby wears oversized bow ties.

Orrin Lieberman. The firm's resident poet. Whenever anyone is stuck for a name for a new corporation, they come to Orrin. When the six Margolis brothers bought a pie company in Dayton, Orrin formed an Ohio corporation and named it 6 M Corporation. Unfortunately, 3 M Company immediately brought an injunction to prevent the Margolises from using the name. Already the Margolises have paid $10,000 in fees to a patent firm in Dayton to defend Orrin's choice. Lieberman is eating hors d'oeuvre and glancing at his watch. He can still catch the 10:36. Cor Bagby is standing with Orrin. He has a Pennsylvania limited partnership that he wants Orrin to name. The general partners are the four Biasi Brothers. Orrin has come up with B-P, Ltd. (Biasi-Pennsylvania). Next week, the Bigelow Pen Company of Cannonsville, Pennsylvania (B-P Co.) will file an injunction against the four Biasis. Orrin is in an unlucky phase. (Corliss will have to face the irate Biasis who, after a four-hour meeting, will rename their partnership P-B Ltd.)

Sean Gillespie Dreyer. Stanford Law Professor. Invited to the party by his former student Marcia Houbignant, who has disappeared with William Toomlin. Ostensibly, Sean Dreyer just dropped into Chicago to check out the North Michigan Avenue galleries for another piece of sculpture for the mezzanine of the law school. He'd like to find a modern version of the Goddess of Justice. Perhaps an aluminum or stainless steel torso and preferably truncated. No head, no blindfold, no arms holding scales. This afternoon, he and Marcia found a burnished-copper female form that would have been great but Sean thought that *"enfin* it wasn't explicit enough." He's wearing aviator-style orange-tinted sunglasses and a short shiny leather jacket and pressed jeans. He stands at the edge of the gathering and tries to find Marcia. He's very casual though, as if he were standing in front of the Union in the main Stanford square, blinking in the bland sunlight.

Deirdre Meyer. Michigan graduate. The first woman to be given quarters in the Gothic rooms of the Law Quadrangle. A vine-covered entrance, a private suite with living room, fireplace, and cork-tiled bedroom. She immediately began an affair with an Iranian engineering student who was waiting tables in the dining hall. He's now a general in the Shah's army and once a year on the anniversary of the founding of the Pahlevi monarchy Deirdre receives a greeting card from Teheran inscribed with the Pahlevi lion, a strand of pearls Scotch taped to the inside of the card. She's received eleven strands since she left Ann Arbor. Tomorrow she's headed for Palm Beach where she'll lecture at a luncheon at The Breakers on Charitable Remainder Trusts. She'll hand carry on the plane sixteen antique silver chambered snail dishes for her restaurant, "La Grenouille," in which she has a twenty percent interest. She stands with her arms folded, the first woman partner in the firm, her hair just giving way to strands of gray. As she notices Hakmir Lhafistan looking for Schloma, suddenly he glances at her and she remembers the young Iranian and her eyes cloud with tears.

Murray Riess. Clerk to a U.S. Court of Appeals judge. Murray was immediately handed a bottle of Scotch in Christmas wrapping as he came into the office. Murray Riess is probably the best opinion writer in the Seventh Circuit. He writes all of his judge's opinions. Mandel Skam, his buddy and clerk to a U.S. District Court judge, was given two bottles and has stashed them under the computer in the Time Room. Murray follows Mandel and slips his bottle under the computer. The two law clerks sit quietly next to the computer in the Time Room watching the dancers through the open doors. The computer lights flash on and off on their faces in the darkness.

Peter Rebeschini and Enid Carlsson are dancing in the library. The two law clerks have opened one of the gift packages of Scotch, and they're getting quietly drunk and very sad watching Enid. She knows they're watching her and she accentuates her dancing with finger snaps and laughter. She also bites her lower lip as she grabs Peter's neck. Mandel lifts the bottle to her in a salute.

Marcia Houbignant and William Toomlin reappear. He's suffered a puncture wound of the right biceps from a dart thrown by Watson Haywood III. Unfortunately, Marcia and Toomlin wandered into Haywood's dark office, where Watts was sitting in his

Eames chair, a bottle of J&B in one hand and a dart in the other. It's a minor wound and Haywood, unconcerned, is still tossing at the board. He did give Toomlin his handkerchief, which Marcia tied into a tourniquet. Toomlin excuses himself and goes to the men's washroom. Marcia finds Sean Dreyer, the Stanford Professor, and they leave. She doesn't know it, but she has several droplets of Toomlin's blood clinging to her stockings.

One of the mailroom boys tentatively leads Marjorie Hackberry out onto the library floor to dance. She is very tall and diffident and snaps her dark glasses down off her hair. She's at least six inches taller. She barely moves.

Corliss Bagby and Deirdre Meyer have finished dancing. She has her plane to catch tomorrow to Fort Lauderdale. Cor Bagby will drive her to her apartment. She would like to say goodnight and thank someone, but the people out on the dark library floor are mostly strangers. She's feeling better now. As she passes the telex, she has the urge to tap out a message to their Washington office. The machine is switched on. She types "P E A C E," pushes the "No Reply" button and leaves. On the way down in the elevator she and Bagby meet Bates-Vonier, who's carrying something about the size of a bowling trophy in a zippered velvet bag. He tips his hat to Deirdre as the elevator doors open at the lobby.

The firm limousine is waiting.

He had gone underground the day after he failed the bar exam. He hadn't thought about it for 30 years, but now, sitting on the flight from Paris to Chicago with the young man beside him studying bar review notes, he closed his eyes and he remembered the pain and how he had immediately gone into hiding.

When the stewardess came around with the wine he nodded pleasantly to the young man. Greenfield held the wine glass up in the beam of his reading light. "À votre sante," he said.

"Santé," the young man answered. "The 'e' is accented."

"I'm sorry, my French is rusty."

The young man didn't smile and returned to his notes.

The kid is really a little shit, Greenfield thought as he looked out the window at the black layers of moonlit clouds. Most of them are insufferable little bastards. They take everything so literally. Had he once been that insufferable? No, he hadn't been that insufferable. He took another sip of the wine.

"Where did you go to law school?" he asked his seatmate with his eyes closed. "I'm a lawyer."

The student, annoyed, put down his yellow marker.

"Stanford."

"My name's Joel Greenfield. I'm a corporate lawyer from Chicago."

"I'm Allan."

"OK—you seem to speak French very well."

"No, I don't speak it well. I hear it well."

"You're studying bar review notes."

The young man began underlining again with his yellow marker and suddenly he stood up, took his knapsack down from the rack, and moved to another seat down the aisle. He turned to Greenfield for a moment. "It's like I don't want to talk," he said, and then slouched down in his new seat.

Greenfield didn't answer him. They were all so goddamned earnest and intense. Had he been that earnest and intense? He'd been loose, casual, graceful, and civilized. He sipped his wine again. He'd known the name of Holden Caulfield's brother, (Allie). No one else in the class knew Allie. No one had even known the name of The Catcher. He also knew that Wallace Stevens, a lawyer, had written "The Idea of Order at Key West," which, gentlemen, more or less explained the universe. It also explained why he hadn't finished two of the questions the first time he'd taken the bar exam and had immediately gone underground for four months.

He looked around the plane and rang the bell for the stewardess. Why not a bottle of Hungarian Tokay and some caviar on those good little crackers Air France served? What was a kid like that doing in First Class anyway? Probably spending more of his parents' money.

He spread the caviar on the cracker and felt the wine beginning to fuzz his mind. It took only about 30 seconds. Everything was absolutely black now out the window. He couldn't tell if he was looking at black clouds or black water.

*   *   *

He wore a black cowboy hat in 1954. He bought it in Amarillo because he knew he hadn't finished the two questions, hadn't even begun the two questions, so he bought a black cowboy hat and wore it home from Amarillo on the trip his parents had given him. Stephen Schwartz's father had bought him a new car and, after the bar, he and Steve had headed west. First, though, they hit St. Paul because Steve knew a girl there. He hadn't told Steve about the two unanswered questions. So he was alone with his shame in St. Paul and with the girl whose face he couldn't remember now. She was still faceless in his memory but he remembered her shoes. Purple suede shoes with brown saddles. Steve was with the laughing, heavy blonde. He remembered the ornate recreation room. Trying to make it with his date on the narrow floral pillowed rattan couch.

And then Omaha, Denver, and across the mountains into New Mexico. Mexican girls in a tavern in the mountains of New Mexico. The sad high-planed serious face of a beautiful Mexican girl. He hadn't bought the hat yet. He bought the hat in Amarillo. Walking the streets of Amarillo in his gray Brooks pinstripe and wearing the new black cowboy hat. It had a red satin lining and the salesman got up on a rolling ladder to bring down the hat box. It was a shiny black box and when he opened it the red lining flashed up at Greenfield like an open wound. All because of two unanswered questions.

Then over the Ozarks slowly heading back to Chicago, wearing the black hat, lighting candles in tiny mountain churches. Kansas City and the hat. St. Louis and the hat and the pale face of his one true law school love who met him in her driveway wearing an engagement ring. She solemnly asked Greenfield into the house. He could see Steve shooting baskets from the window (she'd turned her face away) and he walked back out to the car without looking back at her and roared out of the driveway, jamming into reverse, leaving a rut in her father's expensive pebbles and never once looking back.

He still hadn't told anyone, not Steve, not the Mexican girl, not his lost love in St. Louis, not anyone.

Then Chicago, his anxious parents waiting at the door with the envelope from the board of examiners. Thick, you passed. Thin, you failed. Alone in the backyard with the thin envelope, still wearing the black hat. Had he cried? He couldn't remember now. It had been so long ago.

*   *   *

He poured another glass of wine and looked out again at the black patterns of clouds. Had he cried? What difference did it make? He tried not to look out the window at God's black patterned handiwork. (What if you fell into one of the crevices, where would you wind up? What if the plane burst apart and all of us were cast out like motes adrift in moonlight?) He smiled. He was good at this. Almost as good as Wallace Stevens. He, Joel Greenfield, who flew in and out of Paris now like a weary minister. He, Joel Greenfield, had the same poetic turn as Stevens, even though his tongue was slightly blurred by the wine, just a tad blurred. He, Joel Greenfield, who maintained a farm he'd named Braemor in Barrington with two gun-metal gray Mercedes with "Braemor" incised in tiny white enameled letters on their front doors.

Why should a kid's remark set him off?

It wasn't the remark. It was the attitude. "It's like I don't want to talk." That supercilious attitude.

*   *   *

He moved into the Y on Chicago Avenue and for four months practiced his timing with an alarm clock. Hour after hour, working on his timing against the clock like a boxer. Seeing no one, avoiding his classmates. He disappeared and became a nonperson. When he surfaced for the next examination he was a machine. He finished each question with at least four minutes to spare. As he left the room on the second day, he knew he'd passed. Six weeks later the thick envelope came and he became a lawyer. He went to Springfield with his parents for the investiture and in their album there was still a photograph of him at the base of the statue of the young Lincoln. Soon after the snapshot, he entered his law firm, now four floors of the Bank of America Building, and had simply neglected to mention the failed examination. He said he'd been in Europe at the time of the summer bar and had returned that February. No one had ever inquired further.

*   *   *

Greenfield didn't speak to the young man again until they landed in Chicago. The law student was cleared to San Francisco and remained seated with his notes on his lap as Greenfield stood in the aisle waiting to exit.

"Allan," he said. "Have you ever heard of Salinger?"

"Who?"

"Salinger. Jerome Salinger?"

"No."

"Do you know Holden Caulfield?"

"Does Caulfield teach at Berkeley?"

"Right."

"I don't know him, but my roommate once went to a conflicts lecture Caulfield gave at Berkeley."

"Good," Greenfield said. "By the way," he touched the young man's yellow-lined notes, "good luck."

In the cab on the way to the office Greenfield thought about why they had called him back again. Jack Podhoretz, the chief tax partner, had died, and he'd been called back from Paris to deal with Jack's widow. They had sealed off Jack Podhoretz's office until Greenfield's arrival. He was the only man in the firm who officially dealt with death. He, Joel Greenfield, was the firm's shredder, the one who went in the office and cleaned it up before the family was admitted. He looked for letters, photographs. Anything the family shouldn't see, he destroyed. He was the only man in the firm who specialized in the cosmetics of death. No matter where Greenfield was —Addis Ababa, Hong Kong, Brussels— whenever a man died the door remained locked until he could fly back and go through the office. He knew where to look for the openings, the cracks, the fissures in a man's character. He could find the hidden stack of ancient love letters, the pornographic photographs, the addresses and phone numbers. He was the firm's Catcher in the Rye. As each of them tumbled over the cliff it was he, Greenfield, who stood waiting to catch them and set them back up again. He arranged their last deceit, healed their last wound, covered their one open fissure. After he had finished, the widow could enter the office and lovingly spend days packing her husband's letters and mementos in cardboard boxes.

He dumped his bags and went down to Jack Podhoretz's office and opened the door. He could smell Jack's pipe tobacco. He sat down at Jack's desk. He had the shredder wheeled in by a gray-jacketed clerk. The man left. À votre santé. À votre santé. He still didn't like to be told how to pronounce his French by a punk kid. If the kid was so smart, let him sit in Jack Podhoretz's chair and figure it all out.

He opened Jack's cabinets. Full of unfiled CCH reports. The letters would be close at hand. Probably shoved under the pile of CCH reports. And there they were. He removed a packet of blue envelopes in a delicate handwriting. They were all from the same woman in Albany, postmarked more than 20 years ago. He read one and then ran them all through. He turned them into blue confetti, blue paper ribbons in a plastic bag. They looked like blue entrails in an oxygen tent. The sound of the shredding was barely audible.

Now a photograph. There would be a photograph of her somewhere. Usually in the right-hand drawer, shoved way in back. If the man was right-handed the photograph would be in the right-hand drawer. He found it immediately. Hidden in an old theater program. She was rather pleasant looking, a bright, expectant, round-faced woman. He looked at her and then ran the photograph through the shredder. There was a slight whirring sound. The kid from Stanford with the yellow marker would some day learn about all this and perhaps be not quite so certain. There would be porno too from the last ten years of Jack's life. You can't be an old tax man without turning into a voyeur. Greenfield sat in Jack's chair and looked around. The letter opener. Of course, the handle of the letter opener. If you stood it on point it cast a shadow on the desk of the figure of a young, pubescent girl, perfectly formed. And the boy? Now where was the boy? The scissors, of course. If you stood the scissors on point, the handle cast a shadow of a tumescent boy. He stood the letter opener and scissors side by side on end and smiled. Oh, Jack Podhoretz, you were a foolish man. Where are you, Jack, a mote somewhere in the universe? Alas, poor Yankele. I saved your ass. He would have to take these playthings away. He put them in his pocket. You see, Allan, the fissures a man falls into, the darknesses, the hidden crevices.

THE BALLOON OF WILLIAM FUERST

William Fuerst was very tired. He'd been a lawyer for twenty years and he was very tired. He'd been dragging himself to the office. He could barely make his morning court call. The telephone had become his enemy. The minute he walked into the office the receptionist would hit him with a sheaf of calls. Little urgent notes on red and white message paper. Monday mornings were the worst. All the crazies were waiting for him. The lonely widows: "Oh, Mr. Fuerst, I hope I'm not disturbing you. I had the most awful experience with one of the delivery boys from the drugstore. I gave him a fifteen-cent tip for bringing me a package"—probably a bottle of bourbon— "and he called me a bitch. Now isn't that insolence? Don't you think so? You do think I'm right in reporting him, don't you?"

As soon as he'd hang up and reach for his cup of coffee, the receptionist would hit him again. She knew just when he was at his early morning ebb and she'd let all the crazies come pouring through the switchboard. Finally he'd open his office door and scream at her, "No more calls! Not one, goddammit!"

Then there was the matter of the time book. His was a little black book that he filled with squiggles—time records of his phone calls. After he shut off the calls at the board he'd have to reconstruct time for the time book. It was like taking the calls all over again. "Mrs. Hardiman, .25—call." Fuerst had invented the office decimal system. He remembered when he'd called the special meeting of his partners. He was convinced that a phone call couldn't take less than fifteen minutes. We should keep track of the phone calls at a decimal value of .25. One had to consider the interruption in flow of the lawyer's work, the break in rhythm of the lawyer's concentration. He still remembered his little speech. The way he gracefully used his hands at the conference table, gesturing, holding the red pencil like a conductor's baton. Every call should be treated uniformly as .25. One of the three partners wasn't even recording phone calls. He pointed the red pencil at the offender. He tapped the red pencil impatiently and stared. He was only forty then, still bright-eyed, interested in efficiency. Adamant. At $60 an hour, each call was worth $15. Ten accurately recorded calls a day were worth $150. He smiled at his three partners. That would pay the receptionist's salary for a week. The partners agreed to the Fuerst decimal system. For five years he'd been proud of it. He'd put it across with the red pencil baton like a conductor leading a reluctant quartet, positively, deftly, with graceful gestures. The Fuerst decimal system had worked. Now he was forty-five and very tired. He just didn't give a damn. In fact, his head was leaking time and he was glad about it. He didn't tell any of his partners about the time leak. He always now had the feeling that there was a slight hissing of air from his ears. No one else could hear it, though. A hiss of all the useless acts he performed every day. His vitality, his intelligence, his youth, all being drained away from this secret rent in his head. He knew there was a tiny leak in his head and he'd have to repair it. How to fix it though he didn't know. He'd think about it.

He tried to reconstruct the calls for his time book this morning before he left for the morning court call. There was the woman and the delivery boy. Oh yes, then the man who bought a lemon. The engine was falling out. Some lawyer out in the suburbs had referred him. The man had no money, so Fuerst told him to call Legal Aid or Consumer Fraud. The man called back three more times for advice. He couldn't mark those calls down. Why had he taken them? Why couldn't the receptionist have screened them out?

Then there was the glazier he'd represented in a divorce. Now the glazier was remarried to a younger woman and his first wife was suing for back support. The first wife had taken a lover, though, and they were living in the glazier's house with the glazier's eight-year-old boy. The glazier wanted Fuerst to take the child and the house away. He listened to his client screaming that his ex-wife was a whore. Fuerst hummed to himself and, as the man screamed, doodled patterns— whirlpools of the client's frenzy, circles, triangles, and hexagons. Fuerst could hear a buzz saw in the background cutting glass. Finally the man hung up. When the phone clicked off, Fuerst immediately sensed the hissing sound of air escaping from his ears. He wondered if anyone else heard it. He looked around the office. The stenographers were busy typing. The receptionist was staring at her switchboard.

Fuerst sat down and stared out the window at the lake. The phone rang again. An officer from his bank. Maybe he should put two Band-Aids over his ears to stop the hissing. He took the call from the banker. Fuerst was ten days overdue on his term loan. In twenty years as a lawyer, he'd managed to accumulate a bank debt of $15,000. When he thought about it, he began to sweat. The perspiration was barely perceptible but it was like a fine mist across his forehead. The young man from the bank had been polite: "Perhaps, Mr. Fuerst, there's been a mistake? We haven't received your payment. There was $2,000 due on principal and $950 on interest ten days ago." Fuerst lied to the young banker and told him the check was in the mail. Now the only problem was where to get $3,000? Maybe he'd go to another bank and borrow it. But then he'd have to lie about the $15,000 owed to the first bank because no bank in Chicago would give him another three when he was still out with fifteen. He could just imagine the conversation. Another young loan officer, another pinstriped suit, silk tie, shoes gleaming. "And what did you say you did with the $15,000, sir?"

"Taxes, it mostly went for taxes. And then some remodeling on the house. I don't know. It just grew. But I can handle it." (It was none of this kid's business whether he could handle it.)

Fuerst put his hat on the back of his head and his raincoat over his shoulder and took one more call. He was ready to leave for court. The call was from a man who wanted new instructions in his will.

"I want to be cremated," he said plaintively to Fuerst without saying hello. "And I want it in the will. No urn, Fuerst, do you understand? No *urn*. I want my ashes taken up in a plane and scattered over Lake Michigan. Scattered to the winds. I want my eyes given to Northwestern. I want my heart and my liver given to the University of Chicago."

"I don't know if we can do all that," Fuerst said quietly.

"Why not?"

Fuerst could hear the familiar whine toward frenzy in the client's voice.

"Why not?" the man shouted. "Don't tell me that can't be done. My friends are doing it."

"Giving parts of their bodies away?"

"Everything, hearts, lungs, eyes. What's the big deal?"

"Nothing. I'll take care of it for you." Fuerst hung up. He had a vision of a pilot in an old biplane, struggling with the box containing the client's ashes. The pilot has a white silk scarf streaming around his throat, and, when he tosses the ashes into the slipsteam, they blow back into his face and smudge his immaculate white scarf. Fuerst smiled.

At the courthouse, William Fuerst kept his eye on his hat and coat. They don't teach a course about that in law school. Hat and Coat Watching 103. In the divorce courts in particular it's always important to keep one's hat and coat in full view. Hung out of sight in a back room . . . the lawyer returns from losing a motion at the bench . . . whisk . . . he's also lost his hat and coat. A double loss. So Fuerst sat at the divorce motion call carefully watching the slim tapered obelisk where he'd hung his raincoat and his hat. The clothes post reminded him of the obelisk in the Place de la Concorde and the lawyers scurrying around the courtroom reminded him of automobiles in Paris. No, that was not really true. They reminded him of fish he'd seen in a lagoon in the Florida Keys—barracudas, sharks, stingrays, lethal fish that will prey on you and rip your throat open. They don't teach divorce law either in the law schools, like how to drop $1,000 to a judge's campaign fund. (Drop a dime and make out like a bandit on motions for fees and child support.) Fuerst can remember his constitutional law professor in the wrinkled suit with the glasses on his nose droning on and on for a semester about *Marbury v. Madison*. Nothing about how to schmeer in the divorce courts. Fuerst would drop a dime, too, if he had any money to schmeer. The banks have all his money on overdue notes. Anyway, he was specializing now in keeping his eye on his hat and coat on the obelisk. He couldn't think clearly about bribery. Also there was the matter of the slow leak in his head.

After the divorce courtroom, he walked slowly over to Probate where the judges were more honest but still it was necessary to protect your hat and coat from the lawyers. He hung his raincoat and hat on a Probate obelisk. Here you only schmeered the clerks at Christmas with bottles of Scotch and maybe a box of cigars. There were a few well-dressed women lawyers seated in the courtroom. Fuerst could tell by the exchange of glances between a young woman and an older man that there was a special relationship between them. They were too animated. Her cheeks were flushed. She touched the top of his fingers and swept her hair back over her shoulders and laughed. There was byplay.

Fuerst watched them and then he remembered a young woman at law school. She'd sat next to him in the first semester of contracts and there'd been byplay between them. At least Fuerst had thought so. He remembered her long eyelashes, her reticence, the very pale face and silken auburn hair. Occasionally they'd speak between classes, in the basement with paper cups of coffee. She was having a hard time. She was reluctant to talk about it. She just didn't understand some of the courses. He tried to get her to join a study group, but she never came around. In the second semester she disappeared, and they found her one afternoon in her room hanging from the noose she'd made of her bathrobe cord. She'd stepped off her wastebasket and choked herself to death because she couldn't handle law school.

In those days there was no student health service with therapists. Fuerst had thought that all women law students eventually hung themselves or else became librarians. Then suddenly they reappeared as confident young women with silk bows on their blouses and gold rims around the soles of their shoes. Eyes flashing, some of the young ones had even whipped him badly in argument in the Federal Court. So now, in the Probate Court, he would only nod to the women and sit at one side far away from them, remembering the lovely young girl with auburn hair who stepped off her wastebasket. His eyes were on the coatrack, his hands just playing with the hair at his ears, feeling for the movement of escaping air. His face showed no sign. He had a smile, a confident smile.

After court, he took the elevator down and walked out on the Civic Center Plaza. The sun was beginning to break through the morning fog, and, as he crossed the Plaza, he removed his hat. There was a man in front of the Picasso statue selling helium-filled balloons. Fuerst bought one and a spray can of helium for his youngest child. As he walked back to his office, on impulse he filled the balloon and then, just at the entrance of his building, he let the balloon drift away. No one paid attention to him. He watched the balloon surge up past the girders of a high-rise under construction.

When he returned to his office, the receptionist handed him another sheaf of messages. He carefully hung his hat and coat and went back to his office and closed the door. He tried to see his balloon out the window rising above the Chicago skyline. He couldn't find it. Then it occurred to him that he could patch the leak in his head with the same can of helium he'd used to inflate the balloon. At least he could replace the lost air. He didn't realize that helium would change the timbre of his voice. He gave himself a trial squirt. When the receptionist hit him with the first call back to the new sheaf of crazies, he answered with a high, tiny voice that sounded just like Mickey Mouse.

"Hello," William Fuerst squeaked in the Mickey Mouse voice.

It was the same man who called previously about his ashes. "Is that you, Fuerst?"

"It's me," the Mickey Mouse voice said.

"It don't sound like you."

William Fuerst opened his mouth wide and give himself another squirt of helium. He could feel a slow cessation of the hissing in his head as if the rent were sealing.

"Fuerst. Do you understand? No urn. My ashes. No urn. Do you understand? Get a plane. A pilot."

"I understand," William Fuerst squeaked.

The hissing sound had stopped, though. He held the phone away and felt for movement of air at his ears. There was nothing. He put the client on hold. He knew that if he was silent for a while, the timbre of his voice would return to normal. He dropped the can of helium into his pocket and wondered what would happen if he lit a cigarette. He wanted a cigarette badly but he didn't want to end his career by immolating himself. He couldn't remember whether it was the *Hindenburg* or the *Graf* or was it the *Graf Spee?* Was it helium or hydrogen? He couldn't remember. The phone buzzed again. He gave himself another squirt. "Hello," he answered in the tiny squeaking voice.

"Is that you, Fuerst?"

He put a cigarette in his mouth and struck a match. He held the match in his fingers for a moment and stared at the sudden brightness of the flame and then touched it to the cigarette. Nothing happened. "Okay," he said into the phone, "you have my attention."

THE LAW CLERK'S LAMENT

Mr. Julian Grossman seems to have a fetish for No. 3 Ticonderoga pencils. He saves them and positions them carefully in a sterling silver cup on his desk. When I was hired, he told me one of my duties would be to keep them sharp. I don't sharpen them, though. He insists on doing it. He seems to enjoy standing at the electric pencil sharpener.

I think perhaps there's something sexual about sharpening pencils. You shape the point with exactitude. I mean, you really control that pencil, holding it in the machine until the light glows softly. Grossman likes his pencils spread out in the silver cup, all points up. "Like a Japanese fan," he once said to me.

*   *   *

Even though I have to do ridiculous things like positioning Grossman's pencils in the silver cup, I guess I like my job. The office is only five blocks from law school and I jog over after my morning classes. It's fun to jog in downtown Chicago. I also jog on errands or when I get sent to the Civic Center or the Federal Building to file pleadings. I keep in shape.

Once Grossman insisted I use his pedometer. In one day I put ten miles on it. Grossman wears a pedometer

clipped to one of his trouser loops. You hear him click-
ing when he passes you in the hall.

Another man in the office, Mr. Vance Werner, has
had a heart valve operation and he also clicks when you
stand near him, but it's more like the tick of a fine
wristwatch.

*   *   *

When you enter our office, the first thing you'll notice is
the oiled parquet floor. It almost has the hue of rosewood, or perhaps it's the shadowing in the afternoon
that makes the floor seem to me to be rose colored. The
office is on the seventy-first floor and the light is very
clear in the afternoon.

Mr. Vance Werner once complained that I had
tracked dust into the waiting room. (I wear blue Con-
verse All Stars for jogging and change to loafers when I
arrive at the office.) I had to mop the parquet with an oil
mop to remove the tread marks from my All Stars—
"bunny tracks," Mr. Werner called them.

Vance Werner is a probate lawyer. Every morning
he walks in the door carrying his heavy black satchel.
He drops the satchel on the floor and before he takes his
coat or hat off the receptionist hands him obituary
notices neatly clipped from the morning paper. He
smiles at her. She smiles at him. I think they both
groove on death.

*   *   *

Tonight, on the way home in the North Western station,
as I ran for the 5:45, I noticed they'd installed a new

clock. It's an Accutron and it flashes out the minutes and the seconds. It was 5:43:16 as I passsed.

The guy in front of me who I know from the suburbs used to be an editor of *Chicago Law Review*. He was carrying a briefcase inscribed with the initials of his firm in gold letters. We ran for the train together and he staggered as we hit the stairs. The train was moving as we jumped. I thought for a minute he was going to fall back out the door under the wheels, and I stuck my hand out and grabbed him as the doors hissed shut. He didn't say a word to me. I could see by his eyes that he was really out of it. He just stood gasping for breath on the platform between cars. I wonder if I'll become like this guy in a few years, dazed and burnt out from overwork. I think if I hadn't grabbed him he would have been decapitated.

*   *   *

The men in the office spend an interminable amount of time arguing about money. They're always locking themselves in the conference room. They walk in there grim faced, each of them instructing the receptionist to "hold my calls" or "hold my calls unless it's Mrs. Grossman." I think Grossman is paranoid and that causes most of the problems. He even keeps his symphony tickets locked in a tin box in the vault.

*   *   *

I've a friend who's only a few months out of school. He goes down to the Criminal Court at Twenty-Second and California as a volunteer for the Bar Association. On his "duty day," he'll make $1,000 arguing motions to suppress on narcotics cases.

I went with him one morning last week and listened to the hearings. It was always the same routine. "You have a motion, Counsellor?" "Yes, Your Honor." "Okay, swear the officer." My friend: "All right, Officer, now when you made the arrest and you found this quantity of a controlled substance, you didn't see a sale taking place." "No." "The defendant was just standing on the street." "Yes, sir." "And you made a stop and search." "Yes, sir." "Motion, Your Honor." The Judge: "Granted, discharged. Bond refund $250 awarded to Counsel as fees." To the defendant: "You're free to go, son." The defendant, smiling: "Thank *you*, Judge."

My friend gets the bond refund check in the mail within a week. "No sweat," my friend says. Of course, I notice now he keeps a Colt .45 in his bedroom.

*   *   *

Yesterday morning I went to Federal Court with Mr. De Luria who's a federal defender. He was defending a Mexican guy who was charged with selling heroin. De Luria has a black beard and he always wears the same rumpled pin-striped suit. He's very serious about his work.

The Federal courts have just opened again after being closed for the summer, all of July and August. I suppose the judges need vacations, but it seems strange that the District Court in Chicago should close for two months every summer. What about the defendants who can't make bond and are in the county jail over the summer waiting trial? That place is a hell hole.

The court system is really patrician. You walk into the beautifully panelled courtrooms with handsome portraits of colonial generals on the walls, and all through July and August the courtrooms are empty. De Luria just shrugs when I ask him about it.

Anyway, this morning we had to sit through twenty-five civil motions before they let us see our man. It seemed to me that most of the civil cases didn't have anything to do with notions of justice, mostly fights between insurance companies that should have been adjusted outside the courts. The judge didn't even start hearing motions until two o'clock.

Finally, at eleven they let us go down to the lockup to see the defendant. He was sitting on the concrete floor of the cell with two other Mexicans and they were playing some kind of game with matchsticks. None of them spoke English and they didn't understand anything that was going on. De Luria tried to tell our defendant that he was going to be sentenced this morning and that he'd probably get three years. Finally, De Luria just held three fingers up in front of the bars.

When we got upstairs in the courtroom, they had two other lawyers there for the other two Mexicans, as well as an interpreter. The interpreter was an old guy who was partially deaf, and I don't think the defendants knew what he was talking about. The judge looked tanned and very relaxed in his pleated robe. He listened politely to De Luria's argument in mitigation and then he gave the Mexican three years and a bailiff snapped a pair of cuffs on him and led him away.

De Luria flashed three fingers again but the Mexican kept his head down and wouldn't look back at us. I don't think I'll become a criminal lawyer.

*   *   *

I'm seeing a girl who has an apartment on the North Side. She's a social worker and last night she made dinner for me. I told her about the case but she didn't really listen. She's into the *I Ching,* and after dinner we drank some wine and tossed her *I Ching* sticks. She asked the *I Ching* about the Mexican and it told her that he really was guilty and had even murdered a man in Nogales.

She's very weird. I like her. Maybe someday she'll let me stay overnight, but she always puts me out and I catch the midnight train home. On the midnight train you're in with drunks, sailors, and lots of young lawyers. The lawyers have been down in the big firms' libraries, writing briefs and memos for senior partners. These young guys really look pale and exhausted. I hope most of them make it. I don't know if I'll be able to take that kind of crap.

I had some books with me tonight, so I tried to brief cases, but I fell asleep. And when I got off the train, I walked through the park in the moonlight. I thought about the Mexican and I wondered if he'd fallen asleep or whether he was up and staring out at the moon through his cell window. I thought about De Luria shaking three fingers at him. De Luria's three fingers somehow seemed to be connected with the pencils in Grossman's cup. The pencils are like De Luria's fingers, long and slim and tapered . . . and very useless.

As I walked through the wet grass in my All Stars, I thought of Grossman's Japanese fan fetish and the design of the fan seemed to have a connection with the court proceeding—a very fragile connection.

*   *   *

Joe McElliot keeps a telescope on a tripod in his office. The other day I took a look through it. It's really hard to see anything because your eyelashes get in the way and the image quivers, but apparently McElliot knows what he's doing. When the image finally did come into focus, I was watching a woman in a dressing room on the fifth floor of Marshall Field's.

*   *   *

McElliot always wears a Daley button in his lapel. He says it helps let the judges in the Civic Center know he's one of them. You'd be surprised how many lawyers at the Civic Center wear Daley buttons to court. You get on an elevator in the morning, "Hi ya, Judge," "Hi ya, Counsel," "Hi, Judge," "Good morning, Judge," all of them wearing Daley buttons. His picture is everywhere. The portrait could be of Mao or Tito. Everywhere you go in the Civic Center you see the same portrait, the smiling, benign leader.

In the Civic Center Plaza this morning school children were doing mass gymnastic drills. I stood there and watched the little blonde pigtailed girls and thought how this could have been Berlin in the 1930s and all the unctuous lawyers with their Daley buttons could have been German lawyers laughing together on their way to the morning court call.

*   *   *

Last week McElliot gave me an envelope to take to a man in the assessor's office. I had a feeling there was money in it. I wasn't certain. I tried to hold it to the sunlight that slanted between the buildings as I walked up LaSalle Street. McElliot had inserted a piece of paper and the light didn't penetrate. When I gave the envelope to the guy in the assessor's office, he just grunted. He didn't even look at me.

I think McElliot is into tax defaulted real estate. He pays up defaulted tax installments. So say you're senile or sick and all you have is your pension and your house, and now you can't pay $500 for real estate taxes. You just don't have the money, or maybe you're so senile you don't understand. Well, along comes McElliot, and he puts up his $500 and if you don't pay him back in two years, he gets title to your house and you go on the street. That's the Daley-button system.

I think McElliot is also into fixing taxes. That's probably where the envelope fits in. I think I'm being used as a courier.

I'm glad I tilted his telescope. The next time he looks in it, he'll see the steel mills in Gary.

*   *   *

I had a date last night with a blonde who has an apartment in Evanston, and we went out for some pizza and beer. This girl has very fine cheekbones (I'm a cheekbone man) and long blonde hair that falls across her mouth when you kiss her. She's a poet and a teaching assistant at Northwestern. When I tried to talk to her about the corruption in the Chicago courts, she just laughed and told me, "You're too sensitive to be a lawyer."

She's really into good sex though and I dig that. I think I'm really a lover and maybe I'm not cut out to be a lawyer. I asked her if I could stay overnight and she said "Sure." Just that simple. "Sure."

I made her an omelet in the morning and we jogged together in the little park across the street before we each left for classes.

I don't know, maybe after I finish law school and the bar, I'll leave. Go to San Francisco. Maybe buy a boat and sail the California coast down to Mexico. I'm tired of briefing cases. It's so goddamned boring. I'm also tired of listening to creep law professors.

*   *   *

I wish they'd give me some real law work to do. Today I took the postage meter cartridge over to the post office for a refill.

I went to the bank with the firm's checks, made the deposit and got twenty-five dollars in new bills for petty cash. Grossman insists on new bills. I think he finds a sense of refreshment in touching new money—the same feeling of expiation that a communicant gets when he feels the wafer drop on his tongue.

I delivered a package to a bank trust department.

I picked up some jars of instant coffee and powdered cream.

When I came back to the office, I filed CCH reports.

At 4:30 I had to run an eviction suit over to the municipal court.

The day was really a bummer and at night, when I

got home, I shot baskets in the driveway until I was tired and felt good again. I fell asleep reading the Tax Reform Act.

I like reading taxes—it's all such gibberish, a maniacal kind of geometry. You just click your brain off and let the words run through your mind like snowflakes without trying to make any order out of them—it's like speedreading the Bible. You don't really know what's going on but it makes you feel reverential. I think awe is important to the study of law. You have to be willing to believe without trying to understand.

I'm convinced that man is insane, at least during part of his conscious time, and much of the written law (like the Tax Reform Act) is just a trip into that insane part of man's consciousness. It's like taking a belly flop on a sled out into a vast white snowfield. You slide and slide and slide. Eventually the sled stops and then, if you get off and go have a beer and a few laughs with your woman, you won't think about the snowfield or where you were headed on the sled or what depreciation regulations have to do with the multitude of poor people in this country who urgently require justice.

*   *   *

Grossman is writing a brief and he had me check the cites out before it went to the printer. I pulled each of the volumes down from the library shelves and stacked them in two towers on the conference table and paged each citation. I didn't find any errors, but some of the covers of the volumes are so old that I left fingerprints of leather dust on Grossman's memo. He was really pissed off and now I have to hand-vacuum all the books in the library.

After he finished proofing his brief, he sent a telegram to Shepherd's in Colorado Springs to see if any of his cases had been reversed since the last advance sheets. I had to call in the cites to the Western Union operator. I told her I was really a CIA man and the citations were sort of a code that controlled ICBM silos out in Colorado. She laughed, but I think she probably reported me. I'm not worried. I used Grossman's name on the telegram.

*   *   *

Maybe I shouldn't feel so sorry for the Mexican. I mean, if he really was guilty of selling heroin, he should be in prison. I just wish I knew more about him and then I could come to a reasonable conclusion.

*   *   *

Yesterday afternoon I was sent over on a citation to question a man who owed $125 to a finance company. The office had a judgment against him and he'd been served with a citation and ignored it, so the sheriff arrested him. When the citation cases were called, they brought three men out of the lockup, all in cuffs and all black. None of them owed more than $250, but certain white collection lawyers prey on blacks by using contempt orders to have them arrested.

I saw one of these lawyers file ten contempt petitions. He had them xeroxed. These collection lawyers use the Chicago courts to run their own private debtor's prison. They should be disbarred. I asked the man a few questions, and then I told the judge to discharge him.

The man looked me in the eyes when the bailiff removed the cuffs. I thought he was going to thank me, but he whispered an obscenity and walked out of the court-room. If I keep this up, I might as well get myself a Daley button.

*   *   *

I feel like I'm losing control. I'm being swept into the system. If I don't quit my job, I'll just slide and slide. I'm on the sled headed into that snowfield and I've got to get off. I've got to get off.

*   *   *

Grossman complained again today about the way I had arranged the pencils in his cup. I told him the same obscenity that the black defendant had whispered to me and that of course terminated my job as a law clerk. I don't care. I've got my paycheck, and tonight I'm meeting the blonde in Evanston and we're going to a Woody Allen movie.

*   *   *

I stayed after work to clean out my desk and pick up all my stuff. There was no one there but a scrub woman and, after she left, I put a pot of coffee on and took my cup into the library and sat with the lights off and just watched the city. It's such a magnificent, powerful city, all the gleaming towers brilliant with light, the black-ness of the lake, tiny lights of planes receding into the horizon.

I sat for a while in the dark and then got up and walked around with my cup through the offices for the last time. Very few of the men have anything in their offices that really tell much about them. Grossman has his silver cup, of course, and McElliot the telescope, but most of them have few personal things—perhaps a painting, or a photograph of their wife.

I went into the vault. Someone had left a will drawer open. There were a few hundred wills in the drawer, all stacked in rows of neat white envelopes. They looked like miniature gravestones in a tiny cemetery. Even the two glass panels at the front entrance door, with all the black lettered names of the lawyers, seemed like grave markers in the soft night light. I closed the will drawer and turned off the vault light. Then I left my office key on the ledge at the receptionist's window and sat down and put my All Stars on and went out the door.

I was glad to be leaving. I've realized the men here have lost their connection with the concept of serving people. They're entirely caught up in moneymaking. They aren't really lawyers. They're servants to businesses and wealthy families. I don't want that to happen to me. I don't want to wind up in an office in some city tower, trapped in a glass coffin like the relics of an ancient saint. I don't want to become a money man. I didn't go to law school to become a businessman. The lawyers in this office are like mollusks who've been awash at the edge of the same sea too long. They've become encrusted with their own stagnation and they've lost momentum and direction.

I took the elevator down, and when I hit LaSalle Street the night air felt cool on my face.

I began to jog, a nice easy stride, moving smoothly; weaving through the traffic and all the night people, I felt free again. For the first time in months I knew where I was headed and I was running in the direction of myself. I was no longer a courier for McElliot, or indentured to Grossman. I'm sure they'd both come out of law school with dreams, but they'd corrupted themselves. I am confident that I will not be so corrupted, not as long as I am young and I can run—easily and gracefully— from older men and their wisdom.

She was to become the firm's Jewess. She knew it when they hired her. The hiring committee had been so obsequious and deferential she knew they could hardly afford to let her get away. It was their time for a woman and a Jew, and she fitted both categories.

She was dressed like a woman who had stepped from the pages of *Vogue* into the sparsely furnished conference room of Whitney & Hume the day she appeared before the hiring committee. They were seated before a fireplace framed by natural wood panelling. The fireplace was, of course, artificial, but it was screened and fully ornamented with a brass colonial andiron set. The fireplace ledge held several bone china plates. She wore a black suit with tiny cloth-covered buttons up the sleeves and a brown silk blouse with a single gold chain around her neck. The committee had immediately offered her $50,000 and she had shaken each of their hands and smiled her perfect smile as she measured each of them. O.K. She would be their first Jewess, if that's what they really needed.

Now, two years later, she, just this afternoon, had miscarried a child by John Watson, one of the members of the committee. He'd been seated to her left. She remembered that his hair kept falling over his eyes and he kept pushing it away with his glasses. She

liked his face even then. He'd asked her only one
question.

"Ms. Hirsch, I don't mean to embarrass you or any
of the members of the committee, but this is a question
we always ask each of our female applicants. You are
not now pregnant, are you, Ms. Hirsch? We ask that
because you understand we have work of a magnitude
that requires an uninterrupted work span and preparation for trial. We couldn't have you leave after investing
the time and money that would be required to prepare you."

She thought of asking him whether the question
was also asked of male applicants, whether or not they
were putative fathers. Instead, she answered, "I am not
pregnant." She shook her hair back over her shoulders.
"And if you think I resent the question, I don't."

So she had become the firm's first Jewish associate
and second woman employee. Of course, there were no
blacks or Latins or Orientals. There was a woman
associate in the probate department, Annie Tyler Rod-
man, who was an old spinster. Whitney & Hume, in
Chicago in the summer of 1982, was a rather small firm
with only 65 lawyers. At first they treated her almost
like an exotic hothouse orchid. They gave her a lovely
office and access to an interior decorator. Alison and the
decorator filled the office with Scandinavian furniture,
a teak desk, rosewood coffee table, side chairs with
leather cushions, vases of colored paper flowers,
Marimekko wall hangings and even a small copy of a
Jean Arp sculpture. It was all charged to the firm. The
men would pass and stare at the office and Alison over
their glasses. Some of them would stop and shyly introduce themselves. At first they seemed to her almost

cloned in their three-piece black and gray suits. She was their exotic Jewish bloom, this beautiful young woman whose office looked like a bright garden.

Her affair with John Watson at first began for her as a conscious intellectual choice. She knew the probabilities. He was married, he had a young family, he would never leave his marriage or his young family. He was emotionally connected only to his work. He really didn't need her either as a lover or as a friend. In the early fall they'd been sent to Washington together to conduct depositions. There was late night work, he in his shirtsleeves, she with her shoes off in one of the conference rooms of the firm's Washington office. When they finished, they went to the bar in the Hyatt Capitol Hill for a drink. They ordered champagne at a table, with the lighted white dome of the Capitol shining through the window. It was a beautiful, cool fall evening. There was a small dance floor and he shyly asked her to dance. She remembered the first touch of his face on her cheek. It had begun that simply.

Now, though, having just miscarried his child this afternoon in a game of racquetball, she would tell him at dinner at Akido's. He'd wanted her to have an abortion. He'd implored her to have the abortion. She wanted this child. She even had a name: David Hirsch Watson. But the blob of David Hirsch Watson had come sliding down her leg while she was taking a shower. She had just beaten Heather Jackman three games, slamming the ball against the walls like a wild woman. She felt really good. She knew she was pregnant, it was now almost four weeks since her last period. She'd bought a pregnancy kit and had mixed her urine in it. The ring had been red on the test tube. She'd even begun to wear a red enameled ring on her wedding finger. She stared at the blob on the floor of the shower and the blood glistening inside her leg. It looked like a tiny fetal eye. There was no shape to it, just a piece of slime. She picked it up and got a Ziploc bag from the sandwich counter and dropped the slime of her child in it and put it in the refrigerator behind the stack of rusty V-8 juice cans.

In the Japanese restaurant Alison waited for John Watson and ordered a glass of plum wine from the tiny, moon faced waitress in the kimono. She had the Ziploc bag containing her son in her purse. She would have to arrange for its burial. She hadn't said anything to Heather about the miscarriage, only that she was very tired, when Heather asked why she looked so pale. She watched the waitress mincing her way through the tables. There was a group of Japanese men from a bank seated in the back room. She heard their guttural commands as the waitress handed them hot towels and ceramic jars of sake.

John Watson came in and stamped the snow from his feet. Every time Alison met him, she knew that the affair had to end. It was always a 20-second decision when they met. He was wearing a silly light-weight canvas folding golfing hat and a Brooks gray tweed overcoat. He was tall and slim with clear blue eyes, blonde, with a lean face and delicate features. He looked like a banker or a corporate officer, dressed in a gray pinstriped suit and a thin red silk French patterned tie.

"How do you like this funky old hat," he said as he leaned over and kissed her. He folded the hat and stuck it in his overcoat pocket.

Why did she abide this man, who ordered salad

with no dressing, who asked for water instead of wine, who jogged in sub-zero weather and as he ran pretended to step on the faces of his adversaries in lawsuits. She didn't know. Why did she want his child? Why did she always let him hurt her? How many times had he stared at her with those pale blue eyes and told her that he couldn't be with her, he had to catch the 8:20. He broke their dates so diffidently. Each cancelled meeting, instead of making her angrier, seemed to make him more desirable. The pain had become desirable. It was the only distillate of their relationship, this fine powder of pain. She held to John Watson. She just wanted him available to her. She didn't care about their status. She had even unconsciously begun to dress like him. She began to buy tailored gray woolen suits and subdued patterned silk bow ties. She'd found an Italian gray flannel pinstripe and a navy wool to match his navy wool. She started to order some of her blouses at Brooks and a few button-down oxford shirts with the initials "A.H." on the sleeve.

"You don't like the hat," he said again as he sat down.

"I don't like it."

"You're in a bitchy mood." He pulled his glasses out of their case and put them on and looked at her.

"I don't call this a bitchy mood."

He didn't say anything and calmly began to inspect the menu. "What are you drinking?"

"Plum wine."

"Maybe I'll have a glass of plum wine." He took his glasses off and snapped them back into the case. "And some sashimi—yellowtail."

She was waiting for him to ask her how she felt.

"How do you feel?"

"Fine."

"You look pale. Are you ill?"

"Am I?"

He rubbed his eyes, those cool, blue eyes.

"Okay, you're not ill. There's something I want to say. Are you in a mood to listen?"

"Go ahead." She knew he was going to ask her about the pregnancy.

"The complaint in the Hofstetter case. Alison, you left out five paragraphs in Count I. I had to do the whole goddamned thing over again. That's why I'm late." He glanced at his watch. "It's so damned dark in here I can't see."

"I thought you had one of those glow in the dark things. What happened to your luminous Rolex? I didn't leave anything out, John. The word processor person left it out."

"The word processor person doesn't leave things out. You left it out. You know this is real hardball we're playing. If that complaint went out that way, the judge would think we're fools."

"Are you calling me a fool?"

"I'm not calling you a fool. I'm just telling you, you do it right or you don't do it."

The waitress brought Watson his glass of plum wine and bowed and daintily served it. He tasted the wine and they ordered. Alison didn't answer him.

"All right, let's change the subject." His face was slightly flushed. He looked around the restaurant. He was annoyed to be seen upset in public. She put her purse up on the table and put her chin on it and stared at him.

"I don't want to talk about playing baseball any more, John. I hate those baseball analogies."

He looked down at his plate and then quickly at the couple sitting at the table beside them. He took a small sip of the wine. "Have you done anything about the pregnancy?" he asked quietly.

"I don't know anything about a pregnancy." She pushed her hair back. "Why do you always ask questions in the accusative tense?"

"You know what I'm talking about," he said, looking directly at her.

"I don't want to talk about abortion."

"The firm wants you to terminate this pregnancy, Alison."

"What are you fucking talking about, the firm wants me to terminate this pregnancy?"

"The executive committee wants it done. They know all about it. If you have the abortion, nothing further will be said. Nothing will be done to affect your chance at a partnership. I've been authorized to tell you that."

She didn't answer him for a moment. Then she opened her purse. She held the plastic bag up to the candlelight and watched the liquid slowly flow.

"John, look at this." She tilted the package in the candlelight. The liquid looked like a dull viscous pink jelly. "Do you know what this is? I had a miscarriage. This is it. I had a miscarriage in the shower after racquetball."

"What do you mean?"

"This junk is my miscarriage." She held it up to him again.

"You're carrying it around with you?"

"I wanted to show it to you, so you'd believe me."
She dropped it back into her purse.

He stared at her. "Are you telling the truth?"

"Of course I'm telling you the truth."

He stood up. His hand was trembling. "I want to step outside for a moment." He was ashen. He walked quickly to the front door.

The waitress came with the intricately cut sashimi. Alison stared at the coiled piece of yellowtail in the bed of shredded seaweed that had been set at his place. The seaweed looked like a nest of white tendrils. His coil of sashimi reminded her of something. It was almost protoplasmic, like a cornea surrounded by gel. She stared at it. It looked like the glob in her purse. She removed the Ziploc bag and held it up to the candlelight. All she had to do was replace his coil of sashimi with the coiled glob of David Hirsch Watson and she'd make him eat his own kid. The globs were almost identical, interchangeable. It would be a kind of perverse communion. He was a High Episcopalian and he believed in that kind of communion.

When Watson returned he sat down very straight with both hands on his face. "I'm sorry," he said.

"Are you all right, John?"

"Yes."

"Do you think I'm telling you the truth?"

"Yes."

She looked away for a long moment. "Try your sashimi, John."

He picked at the coiled eye of gel with his fork and held it up and then swallowed a piece of it.

"How is it?"

"It's okay."

"I'm glad you like it."

He took a second piece in his fork and finished it and drank some of the plum wine.

"You just ate your kid, John."

"Yes," he said.

"Did you hear what I said?" She pointed her finger at the empty nest of shredded seaweed. "You just ate your kid."

He touched the edges of his mouth with the stiff corner of the scalloped napkin.

"That wasn't sashimi."

"Oh."

"You want to play hardball, John? Like they do in the men's games?" She stood up and began to walk away.

"Sit down, Allie."

She was standing over him, her purse held tightly under her arm. She was angry but not crying. She could cry later. She wasn't going to let herself cry here, in front of him. She carefully went for her coat. She didn't want to faint. It was a black coat, with a small mink collar. She shook out her hair and returned to him and slowly put it on.

"Sit down, Alison."

"No, I'm going. The sashimi. It wasn't sashimi. I replaced it with our fetus, our child."

"What are you talking about?"

"Okay, it wasn't our fetus. It wasn't a fetus. It was our glob. I put it on your plate and you ate it. You ate our kid."

Suddenly his eyes narrowed and he grabbed her wrist. The recognition of the horror of her act had come to him. She yanked her arm away and ran toward the door.

"You Jewish bitch!" was the last thing she heard him scream at her. Her wrist was bleeding where her bracelet had cut into her as she wrenched her hand free.

*   *   *

Later in the park she dug a hole in the ground beside the Grant Park Pavilion opposite the Art Institute with a hand hoe she bought at a drugstore. She'd begun to cry now for the seed growing inside her with the feeling of a soft dark flower. On her knees she dug the hole deeper. Was it beginning to snow? The ground was so hard. She looked around. She didn't see anyone. She should stop crying so she could see someone. She could be raped or mugged out here alone in the park. She'd run her stockings and there was mud smeared over the panels of her coat. She had a deep cut where he'd grabbed her wrist. She removed the bag from her purse and opened it and poured the gel into her hand. It looked like a tiny eye, a tiny dull eye, the slime of their child. She dropped the slime into the hole she'd dug. Of course she hadn't fed him their child. Let him think she'd done it. She wasn't courageous enough to do something male and civilized like that. On her knees she patted the dirt with the hoe and then stood up and stepped on the earth, tamping it down gently.

THE JUDGE'S CHAMBERS

He was a judge of the United States District Court for the Southern District of New York. His name was William Frederick Gottlieb and he had been on the District Court bench in New York for forty years. He was now seventy-five and this year had voluntarily removed himself from active status to the less arduous duties of senior judge. As a senior judge he was given a reduced court call. Instead of presiding over two hundred cases, his call was limited to fifty. He was also given a smaller courtroom.

Each morning he arrived in his chambers at precisely 9:40 a.m. He lived in a suburb on Long Island and he rode the 7:48 commuter train, a rather leisurely ride, arriving at Grand Central twenty minutes or so later than the express trains. He avoided the express trains and the rush hour crowds. He liked to read the *Times* on his way into the city and then nap for perhaps fifteen minutes. He always took a cab to the courthouse. The fare was $1.25 and he gave a quarter tip. At 9:37 he'd step off the elevator and at 9:40 he'd walk through the glass doors of the private judges' entrance, nod to the uniformed guard, and stroll down the long gray-carpeted corridor to his chambers.

Although his new chambers were smaller, he'd kept most of the furniture he'd used in the larger quarters.

He had a massive, varnished mahogany desk with a long conference table perpendicular to the desk. Three highbacked green leather swivel chairs were placed at each side of the conference table. The chair behind his desk was black leather, larger than the green ones; it was a presiding judge's chair his wife had found in an antique shop in Boston. He'd sat in that chair as judge for forty years; the leather was sketched with the silhouette of his body like the angel-wing imprint a child leaves in fresh snow.

Before going on the bench each day Judge Gottlieb liked to have a cup of coffee as a quick stimulant. It seemed to clear his head and give him energy. His clerk served the coffee in a white-enameled mug that bore a presidential seal. The mug had been given to the judge by Franklin Delano Roosevelt in 1937. Fred Gottlieb had been a young partner in a Wall Street firm that contributed heavily to Roosevelt's campaigns. He was thirty-five when FDR made the appointment and the rumor on the Street was that his appointment had cost his firm at least $100,000. If indeed that fact were true, the judge would have been presented with a very expensive coffee cup. The truth, however, had long been laid to rest with FDR's death and the death of Fred Gottlieb's senior partners. The judge himself was the only survivor.

Recently Judge Gottlieb had been having slight dizzy spells. There were moments when he experienced lightheadedness. He could tell when they were about to come on: there would be a tingling sensation in his arms and legs and then the fuzziness would seep into his head. When he had one of these attacks, whatever he was reading would blur and his head would swell, his speech becoming tangled and disembodied. Then the dizziness would sweep over him. Sometimes he felt as if there were a presence on the crown of his head, a weight, numbing and yet comforting.

He would try to ignore the symptoms. Usually, by the time he entered his chambers, whatever early morning discomfort he'd experienced—a slight spell on the train or at breakfast—would have dissipated. This morning he felt fine. He was fresh and eager to get to his court call. First, though, he unwrapped the package that his wife had sent from Tiffany's. He knew it would be another wirehaired terrier. His wife, for some reason, had become fixated on statuettes of wirehaired terriers. He must have had twenty spotted around, on his desk, the conference table, the end tables at the couch, his window sills. He wished she would stop sending the damned wirehaireds.

He got up and walked toward the door that led from his chambers to his courtroom. He pushed the button on his digital watch: 9:58. His wife would be . . . at the grocer's. No, no, at the butcher shop. What day was it? Monday. Or was it Tuesday? The thirteenth? The fifteenth? Saturday was the eleventh, so if today was Monday, it would be the thirteenth. His wife's face came clearly to him now; she was in bed having an egg in a cup. He smiled. Of course today was Monday the thirteenth and at 10 in the morning she'd be sitting up against two pillows with her sleep mask strung around her neck, cracking an egg with the little souvenir spoon, the spoon he'd brought home from Portland, Maine, the year he met Harry Hopkins. Was it 1934? The handle was inlaid with tiny pearls and the spoon was fluted and incised with a rose heart that glowed when you held it up to the light. He could hear her tapping her egg . . . tap, tap, tap; she always used three quick little blows, increasing the strength of each just slightly and with the third severing the dome of the egg.

He was on the bench now and the gavel was rapping. "Hear ye, Hear ye, Hear ye. The United States District Court for the Southern District of New York is now in session, the Honorable William Frederick Gottlieb presiding. All those having business before the court please be seated and remain quiet." The gavel rapped again. "God save the United States and this Honorable Court."

He shook his head. His wife's face disappeared. Instead there were two eager young lawyers approaching the bench. "77 C 3487, *The United States of America v. Joaquin Mendoza Lopez,* arraignment and plea." His clerk had called the first case and handed him the index card. A door opened at the side of the courtroom and a large black bailiff escorted the prisoner Lopez to the bench. Lopez was dressed in an orange jumpsuit, prison issue, and Judge Gottlieb looked down at him through his reading glasses. A young, handsome Spanish face. Who did he resemble? Was it Rudolph Valentino? No, of course it wasn't Valentino; this boy's face was heavier. This face, the face of the prisoner Lopez, was it the young Picasso? Where had he seen a photograph of the young Picasso? At the Metropolitan, at the Frick? No, it couldn't have been the Frick. "Casals," he said to the woman interpreter. "Pablo Casals."

"No, Your Honor, Joaquin Lopez." She smiled a bright little smile.

"Of course, Lopez," Judge Gottlieb said. "Joaquin Lopez." Gottlieb pronounced Lopez with a Castilian lisp on the Z sound. "Have you been sworn, Madam Interpreter?"

"I have, Your Honor." Her dark eyes flashed at Gottlieb.

"Good morning, Your Honor. Peter Eckelson from the Federal Defender office representing the defendant."

"Good morning, Counsel."

"Elliot Wagner representing the United States, Your Honor."

"Good morning. Does the prisoner waive the reading of the indictment?"

"Yes, he does, Your Honor."

"All right, how does he plead?"

"He pleads not guilty."

"I will set this for status September 14. Twenty days for motions."

"If it please the court," the young lawyer, Eckelson from the Defender's office, was speaking. "There's a $10,000 bond here. I would like to ask that it be reduced to a $5,000 O.R. bond at this time. The defendant has no previous record. He has a family, a wife and child. He's a barber and there's employment waiting for him. His uncle lives here in Queens and is a self-employed businessman and is willing to assist."

"I'm sorry," Judge Gottlieb said. "Mr. Lopez"— the Castilian Z again—"is accused of having sold a rather substantial amount of heroin. Under the circumstances, I will not reduce the bond." The bailiff touched Lopez lightly on the elbow. Gottlieb's clerk immediately called the next case.

"77 C 1228, *The United States of America v. Eduardo Sanchez,* motion for stay of mandate." Gottlieb's clerk took pride in his ability to call the next case exactly at the moment the judge had rendered a final decision. The rapid call of the case immediately cleared the floor. Two new lawyers approached the bench; a new index card was handed up.

Eduardo Sanchez was ushered out of the lockup into the sudden brightness of the courtroom. He was wearing the same type of orange-colored jumpsuit and the same bailiff stood behind him.

Gottlieb thought that the prisoner Sanchez looked like the young cadet in a painting by Francisco Goya, a slender boy cannoneer standing in a plumed hat and a cannoneer's crossed belts and boots. The judge noticed the way the sunlight touched upon the high planes of the young man's face.

"Susan Epstein from the Federal Defender Office representing the defendant, Eduardo Sanchez."

"Elliot Wagner for the United States."

Where had he seen Susan Epstein's face before? The Modigliani portrait of the sculptor, Jacques Lipchitz, and his wife? Of course. Susan Epstein resembled the wife. The same quadrants of the tilted plump face, the hair caught in a bun, the white shawl collar.

Suddenly it seemed to Gottlieb that the proceeding before him was really just a painting of a courtroom scene, that all the participants were unreal. The boy Goya figure. The woman defender with the Modigliani face. The prosecutor—was the prosecutor real? Susan Epstein was speaking. The left side of Gottlieb's mouth opened and a strand of drool slid down his chin. He wiped the saliva away unconsciously with his handkerchief.

Susan Epstein looked up at Gottlieb.

"Young lady."

"Your Honor?"

"Do you know Rembrandt's last name?"

"Sir?"

"Van Rijn," Gottlieb said.

"Sir?"

"I asked if you know the last name of Rembrandt."

"I do not, Your Honor."

"Van Rijn."

"Yes, sir."

Gottlieb nodded his head and straightened the papers before him. He squared them into a neat little pile and glared at the young woman lawyer.

His two law clerks were seated in the jury box, two young men, graduates of Columbia and Yale. He looked over at them. One of the law clerks stood up in the jury box.

"Your Honor," he said, "were you speaking to us?"

Miss Epstein turned to face the clerk.

"Young lady, don't you turn your back on me," Gottlieb said curtly to her. "Face the court at all times."

"I'm sorry, sir," she said.

"You should be," Gottlieb said.

The law clerk was still standing in the jury box.

"Sit down, young man," the judge called out to him, and the clerk sat down. "Take the defendant back to the lockup, Mr. Bailiff. This discussion does not concern him. He may return when I call for him."

"Yes, sir." The bailiff took Sanchez by the elbow and guided the prisoner away from the bench back to the door at the side of the courtroom.

"Now, then, Miss Epstein." The left side of the

judge's face felt frozen, as if it had been filled with novocaine. There was a ringing sensation in his left ear and a blurring of vision. "Now then, Miss Epstein . . . now then, tell me, if you can, the true surname, or the Christian name, of the Spanish artist El Greco."

"Your Honor, I do not know the name of El Greco."

"Domenico Theotocopuli."

"El Greco, Your Honor."

"Yes, young lady. El Greco. Domenico Theotocopuli."

"I see."

"But you don't see."

"I think I do."

"I don't think you do. You may stand down."

The young woman turned from the bench and walked back to the counsel table.

"Bring the prisoner back out," Judge Gottlieb instructed the bailiff.

"77 C 1228, *The United States of America v. Eduardo Sanchez,*" the clerk called out again.

The prisoner Sanchez was brought before the bench. Miss Epstein returned to the bench and stood beside Sanchez.

"You are Mr. Sanchez," Judge Gottlieb said to him.

The prisoner did not respond.

"You are represented by this young lady?" Gottlieb pointed at the federal defender. "You are seeking a stay of mandate?" Gottlieb paused while the interpreter whispered to the prisoner. "Mr. Sanchez, you are accused of entering the United States illegally. This is your second offense. Why is a stay of mandate desired in this case?"

Miss Epstein spoke. "Mr. Sanchez is married to a woman in Yonkers who is pregnant. The child is due any day. The pre-sentence investigation shows that the defendant is a good father, has always held down a job, in fact two jobs, Your Honor. We feel it would be beneficial for the mother and marital relationship if the defendant could be kept here, Your Honor, perhaps in a work-release program rather than have him incarcerated upstate where he'll be separated from his family. We ask that the mandate be stayed at least until the mother and child leave the hospital and arrangements can be made for their care."

"Denied," Judge Gottlieb said.

"Your Honor?"

"I said denied, young lady."

"Yes, Your Honor."

"The defendant Eduardo Sanchez has been previously sentenced by this court to two years in the federal penitentiary and three-years probation. In the event the defendant shall ever return to the United States after his incarceration, the three-years probation shall be revoked and he shall serve an additional three years in the penitentiary. The Motion to Stay Mandate is denied."

The bailiff took Sanchez's elbow again, and, as they turned away, Sanchez stopped and held his hands out to the interpreter and said something to her. She shook her head but he approached the bench anyway. She stood with him and listened and then translated for the court. Sanchez was pointing to the seal of the

United States above the bench, the eye radiating in a triangle above a pyramid. He spoke to the interpreter and jabbed his finger up.

"He says, Your Honor, that you sit below the sign of the evil eye." She pointed to the seal. "That you should be careful that it does not cast a spell on you and affect your judgment. It is a magic sign." She shook her head at Gottlieb as if to negate the prisoner's statement or at least disassociate herself from it.

Gottlieb was standing now. "Madam Interpreter, the defendant's remarks will be noted." He looked down at his court reporter. "Also, Miss Epstein, perhaps you and the interpreter will inform the prisoner Sanchez that under ordinary circumstances the court would consider his remarks contemptuous, but the court takes into consideration the defendant's lack of education and also his inability to deal with the English language and the judicial system of our country." Gottlieb cocked his head at the seal above him and the inscription "Annuit Coeptis Novus Ordo Seclorum." He remembered FDR laughing as he handed Gottlieb the coffee mug with the Latin inscription.

"Hopkins made it up. This year begins the new secret order."

Judge Gottlieb spread his robed arms out toward his clerk. "In any event, Miss Epstein, if it is an evil eye, its magic has now been worked on Mr. Sanchez." The judge smiled. The clerk looked up at Gottlieb who nodded and the clerk rapped once sharply with his gavel. Gottlieb slowly walked down off the bench into his chambers, steadying himself with his hand on the wall as he descended the two small stairs that led from the bench. The clerk rapped again after the door to the chambers had closed.

Still in his robe, Gottlieb settled back into his chair behind his desk. He rubbed the left side of his face and straightened the new statuette of the wirehaired terrier his wife had sent that morning. Then he poured himself a cup of coffee in the mug FDR had given him. The cup was warm and reassuring in his hand. He extended his forefinger to the worn pattern on the cup, the eye radiating from the triangle. He touched the eye and then he touched the same finger to the side of his face where the pain had been. They have such certainty, these young people. Such rectitude. He touched the eye and then his cheek again and waited for his mind to clear so he could remember his phone number and call his wife.

ABOUT THE AUTHOR

Lowell B. Komie is a Chicago attorney and writer. He received his B.A. from the University of Michigan in 1951 and his J.D. from Northwestern University in 1954. His stories have appeared in *Harper's, Chicago Magazine,* and *Student Lawyer,* the magazine of the Law Student Division of the American Bar Association, and in university and literary quarterlies.